Late-Blooming Flowers

ANTON CHEKHOV

LATE-BLOOMING FLOWERS

and other stories

Translated by I. C. Chertok & Jean Gardner

CARROLL & GRAF PUBLISHERS, INC.
New York

First Carroll & Graf edition 1984.

Carroll & Graf Publishers, Inc.
260 Fifth Avenue
New York, N.Y. 10001

ISBN: 0-88184-029-7

Manufactured in the United States of America

Contents

Introduction

This is a collection of Chekhov's newly translated stories: his first long one, never before published in the United States, "Late-Blooming Flowers" of 1882, his last one, "The Fiancée" of 1903, and six others written at intervals between. We have aimed at a selection which would be harmonious in style and theme, one which, in Grigorovich's words,[1] would "take in the motif of love, with all its subtlest and most secret manifestations." The stories are not too well known here, and for the most part have not been translated into English for more than forty years.

The title story, one of Chekhov's longest, appeared in four installments from October 10 to November 11, 1882, when Chekhov was twenty-two, in the magazine *Mirskoy Tolk'* (*Talk of the Town*), a Moscow weekly journal, under the editorship of N. L. Pushkaryov, devoted to literature and political comment. "Late-Blooming Flowers" came out in numbers 37, 38 and 39 of the magazine and concluded in number 41, with an unex-

[1] See Notes to "Verochka," p. 238.

plained omission from number 40. It was signed A. Chekhonte. As the Notes to the posthumous Soviet edition show (p. 235) the original manuscript was considerably worked over, probably by Pushkaryov, a writer himself, who probably had not much confidence in the style of his young contributor.

Mirskoy Tolk' had a circulation of between 2,500 and 3,000, rather small for the time, and it failed about a year later. There is no mention of the story in the Moscow literary criticism of the day for reasons we can only conjecture. Its serialized publication, covering almost five weeks, may have been against it; or the feeling of most editors then that Chekhov's forte was the short, even the very short story; or perhaps the politically dangerous portrayal of an aristocratic family, for the Tsar Alexander II had been assassinated a year before, in March 1881, and it was a period of sharp reaction and stricter censorship. In fact a year later, in 1883, several of Chekhov's stories were suppressed altogether by the censor.

Chekhov was at that time beginning his fourth year of medical school at the University of Moscow (he graduated in June 1884), living with and largely supporting his impoverished family, sharing a room with his elder brother, Nikolai, and his younger brother, Mikhail. (Nikolai, a painter of decidedly bohemian habits, died of tuberculosis in 1889; Mikhail also became a writer, and with their only sister, Marya, took over the administration of his famous brother's literary estate after his death and wrote a very informative biography of him in 1937, a year before his own death.) To add to the atmosphere of perpetual open house in the crowded run-down apartment, Chekhov had brought two fellow medical students with him from his home town in the south, Taganrog. A third medical student, Nikolai Ivanovich Korobov, whose father for some reason considered the Chekhov household a good environment for him, had arrived from Vyatka and the three youths were living with the family as paying boarders. Chekhov and Korobov became close friends and remained so till the end of Chekhov's life, and "Late-Blooming Flowers" is dedicated to him. The character of Toporkov is partly based on one of their professors at the University Medical School, the famous G. A. Zakharin, an eminent diagnostician and one of the greatest clinicists of his day, who was also renowned among the students for the pomposity of his manner and his businesslike attitude toward his profession.

This story, like "A Visit to Friends" and the unfinished "A Reward Denied," was not included by Chekhov himself in his collected works published shortly before his death, nor in any of the earlier collections. Perhaps he did not regard it as a serious or typical piece of writing. Yet although it is rather conventional in treatment and plot in marked contrast to his later work, sometimes awkward in style and studded with clichés, there are unmistakable touches of the master's hand in it, scenes and comments that he alone could have written. Who can forget Toporkov's waiting room, or the vivid descriptions of the approach of autumn, winter, spring, or the Princess's tea party for the doctor? It also displays very clearly the author's dramatic gift, for each of the three long chapters ends on a natural curtain and is divided into clear-cut "scenes" which, with hardly any changes in dialogue, could be staged almost as written.

The idea of marriage for money, incidentally, was unpleasantly familiar to him, for at the time both his mother and his father were urging him, as they did for years after, to marry a merchant's daughter and settle down in comfort. The romantic and idealistic young Chekhov did not encourage their hopes, and indeed he successfully resisted the idea of marriage itself until two years before his death. Chekhov's attitude to marriage was expressed very clearly in a letter he wrote years later to his friend Suvorin: "I could not endure the sort of domestic bliss that goes on from day to day, from morning till night; I promise to be a splendid husband, but find me a wife who, like the moon, would not shine in my heaven every day."

During the whole time of his medical studies, from 1879–1884, Chekhov wrote constantly, and from the time of his first acceptance by the humorous magazine *The Dragonfly* in 1880 until he began to establish his

reputation about the year 1886 he contributed to upwards of a dozen journals under as many pseudonyms
—A Man without Spleen, The Nettle, Ulysses, The
Prosaic Poet, The Blockhead, The Cricket, for example
—apart from his most famous one, Antosha Chekhonte,
the nickname given him as a boy by his scripture
teacher. Even his closest friends did not know all his
identities. His early stories usually dealt with traditional
topics—weddings, holidays, festivals, summertime—or
were very short one- or two-page "jokes," which many
editors preferred. As a schoolboy in Taganrog he had
edited a handwritten, largely humorous magazine called
Zaika (*The Stutterer*) and forwarded copies to his elder
brother, Alexander, who had preceded the family to
Moscow. Alexander praised his efforts highly and showed
them around to various editors he knew. Some of these
schoolboy "jokes" were apparently published, but no
trace of them remains except in Alexander's letters.
"Your anecdotes will go into *The Alarm-clock*," a humorous magazine, he wrote him in 1877. "Two of them
are very good, the others rather weak. Send more short
and sharp stories; the long ones are colorless." *Long and
colorless* was a phrase re-echoed by editors over the next
few years. "Like one of those white paper streamers a
conjuror keeps pulling out of his mouth," as one editor
unkindly put it. His material would sometimes lie
around in editorial offices for months, and then often be
printed with altered endings. However, in spite of these

rebuffs, the pressure of his medical studies, and the first indications of tuberculosis, Chekhov continued to write and, in Korobov's words, "his earnings served as the chief support of his impecunious family."

The second story, "The Little Trick," is a fast-moving vignette, told almost entirely in the present tense. As the Notes show (p. 236), in revising it for the collected works Chekhov put in a completely different ending from the original, sadder but certainly more probable. Here we have a theme many times repeated in his later work, that of a girl who seeks love and offers it, a man who rejects and flees from it. In "Verochka," written a year later in 1887, the theme is explicit. By this time Chekhov had been signed up as regular contributor to Alexander Suvorin's famous newspaper, *Novoye Vremya* (*New Times*), in which both "Verochka" and "The Beauties" first appeared. He now signed his stories in his own name and had begun to enjoy a real and growing fame.

"The Beauties," one of his most evocative stories, written in a poetic and lyrical Russian, demonstrates the new maturity of his style, a style he worked on ceaselessly. Indeed it is startling to read in the Notes how tirelessly, even to the very end of his life, Chekhov worked over and rewrote, cut and changed, shifted commas and altered subjunctives. This very short story is a paean of praise to that special, brief and haunting beauty—first as a boy sees it, then as a man—that one encounters here and there, very rarely, and only in a young and quite unspoilt girl.

By 1893, when "Big Volodya and Little Volodya" was published, Chekhov was an established writer and had paid off many of his debts; he had made his visit to the convict settlement of Sakhalin in 1890, and in 1892 had bought a country estate at Melikhovo, two-and-a-half hours by train from Moscow. Yet it seemed to be a low point in his life and during the winter of 1893–1894 it was even rumored among his friends in St. Petersburg that he was dying of consumption, although Chekhov strenuously denied it. (In a letter to Suvorin in November 1893, he wrote: "My cough has grown worse, but it is still a long way from consumption . . . I haven't had a discharge of blood from my throat for a long time. Why Leykin is spreading all these strange and unnecessary rumors in Petersburg only God who created fools and gossips knows.") Whatever the cause, this story reflects a dark and hopeless mood in which, apart from the heroine's personal tragedy, Chekhov shows his contempt for the empty, useless life of the women of his day, particularly the women of the upper classes for whom his Sonya sees no choice but the death-in-life of the convent or her own hysteria and despair.

This was a favorite theme of Chekhov's and one where he found it hard to restrain his natural preaching instinct, for there has seldom been a writer so bored by domesticity as Chekhov. To his hero the sight of Tatyana in his next story, "A Visit to Friends," presiding at the family table, eulogizing her "nest" (a word he often used) was not natural but on the contrary against reason. Why should she be wasting her time like this? In fact, Podgorin's view of the family scene, though not an unappreciative or an unsympathetic one, is essentially that of an outsider.

"A Visit to Friends" was written in the winter of 1897 in Nice, where Chekhov, after the critical failure of his first full-length play *The Sea-Gull*, had gone to recuperate from a violent attack of his old sickness. In his charming letter to the editor of the magazine *Cosmopolis* which had requested an "international" story from him (see Notes, p. 243) Chekhov said: "I could only write a story like that in Russia, from memory. I can only write from memory, I have never written directly from life." Certainly this story, which as he says he wrote "slowly . . . and with some difficulty" is steeped in the very atmosphere of a Russian summer in the country, and in some aspects resembles *The Cherry Orchard*. It contains a superbly analytical portrait of the young lawyer, Podgorin, who like Ognev in "Verochka" and Lopakhin in *The Cherry Orchard* lacks the courage or even the will to accept love when it is offered to him.

The next story, "A Reward Denied," which was never finished, stands quite apart from all the others translated here. We know very little about "A Reward Denied," published posthumously in 1905, except that it dates from the year 1902–1903, i.e., after the successful production of *Uncle Vanya* in 1900, *The Three Sisters* in January 1901, and his marriage to the actress Olga Knipper, who played leading roles in both plays, in May 1901. Chekhov spent several weeks in the summer of 1902, and again later, at Stanislavsky's *dacha* Lyubimovka, near Moscow. Stanislavsky's mother was very pious and there were services nearly every day, so it is possible that the atmosphere so well described in the Bondaryov household may have been partly drawn from Lyubimovka.

As we can see from the notes to "A Visit to Friends" and "The Fiancée," Chekhov was in the habit of selecting titles for his stories before he finished, or sometimes even started on them, and he attached importance to them. In this case we have to guess what the title implies; *Rasstroistvo Compensatzii* means literally *Destruction of Compensation*. We have only two chapters of the story and we shall never know what happened when Vera Andreyevna's unnamed lover returned from Italy, or if Yanshin "even for an hour" succeeded in breaking out of his oyster shell. It is a severe loss to be cheated of the last chapters of a masterpiece, for in confidence and strength of style and in richness of content we see Chekhov the storyteller at the height of his powers here.

Introduction

His last story, "The Fiancée," published in *Zhurnal d'lya Vsyekh* (*Journal for Everyone*) in December 1903, was also his last work except for *The Cherry Orchard*. As the Notes show, it was written over several months from October 1902 to the end of February 1903, begun in Moscow and finished in Yalta. Chekhov made a start on *The Cherry Orchard*—first the title, which he wrote down several days before anything else— shortly before finishing the first draft of "The Fiancée," but did little more on the play until July, when he and his wife returned to Yalta from Moscow. In the interval between February and July, Chekhov made innumerable changes in the proofs of "The Fiancée." And this was in the last stages of his illness when, with only a year to live, he was so weak that he often could not write more than half-a-dozen lines a day.

He concealed the story from his wife and his family as long as he could, knowing how it would upset them, for in Sasha he has drawn a scarcely disguised self-portrait. Nadya, on the other hand, is one of those young, intensely feminine girls he celebrated, whom we immediately think of as a typical Chekhov heroine. Like Princess Marusya in "Late-Blooming Flowers," Nadya is tall, slender, beautiful, well-bred, and spirited but at the same time gentle, with large eyes and generous emotions, the very picture of Chekhov's ideal, in art as in life. For although he was chivalrous and open-minded in his views on women, opposed their incarceration in the home, and would not let his wife give up her stage career for him, whenever he sketched one of the "new women" it is plain he did not much care for them (the coarse, masculine Rita of "Big Volodya and Little Volodya," for instance, or the pathetic, emancipated Varya in "A Visit to Friends"). Nadya is an attractive and touching portrait, but her conversion is not entirely convincing.

Sasha, however, is a deeply conceived character into which Chekhov has written his last philosophic message. He stands off and smiles with tolerant irony at Sasha's vision of the future but does not renounce it, for this is the same Chekhov who as Stanislavsky says, displayed "his childlike joy when I told him about the big house going up on a Moscow square on the site of a wretched one-story dwelling which had been taken down"; the same Chekhov who wrote in his notebook "What a good thing it would be if each of us left behind him a school, a well, or something of the sort, so that our lives should not pass by in utter oblivion." In spite of his imperfections, Sasha—who, like Chekhov himself, dies uncomplaining, joking, full of hope—is a character of real strength, profoundly revolutionary, obsessed with a determination to change the very direction of human life. Sasha wants to "transform" Nadya's life, or in the Russian verb *perevernut*, which literally means to turn upside down, or right around. Much has been said by the Russian critics of his day, particularly Gorky, about

Chekhov's fight again *poshlost'* which is often inadequately translated into English as "vulgarity." But it was not vulgarity, in the ordinary meaning of the word, that he opposed so bitterly—it was the many other meanings of *poshlost'*: banality, stupidity, triviality. He opposed the hypocrisy, insensitivity and greed that smother the hope of a nobler future; he opposed the unregarded cruelty of his time. And he was not patient in this, he wanted "that new life . . . to come faster." As he complained to Gorky, "We say to ourselves: it'll be better under a new tsar, and in two hundred years it'll be still better, and nobody tries to make that good time come tomorrow . . . people get more and more stupid, more and more isolated from life, like crippled beggars in a religious procession."

His own life was a never-ending battle against oppressive odds—poverty and debt, family cares, even heredity (he liked to joke about "the lazy Ukrainian blood that flows in my veins") and, above all, increasingly severe and, as he well knew, incurable disease. Just as Sasha lectures Nadya, so Marusya twenty years before had lectured the wretched Georges and Chekhov himself, in letters of many numbered paragraphs, had lectured his elder brothers Alexander and Nikolai for their drinking and the waste of their talent. No one saw the human condition more clearly or judged it more realistically than Chekhov, yet he believed to the end that not only the circumstances but the very nature of human life itself could be improved and that it was the duty of men and women to improve them both.

Far from being the melancholy apologist of decadence and despair, as he is still too often pictured, Chekhov was a writer who desired change passionately and fought for it—as he said to the young student Alexander Tikhonov in 1902, his aim in writing his plays was to make people realize how bad and how boring their lives were.

In Trofimov, the "perpetual student" of *The Cherry Orchard*, whose comically high-minded view of the glorious future is challenged by Lopakhin, Chekhov gives a moving answer to the sceptical, the cynical, the lazy: "I shall get there. (pause) I shall get there, or I shall show others the way to get there."

From the second proofs (see Notes, pp. 247–249) we see that he made some interesting alterations to the last chapters before the final printing. The original second draft had a more politically revolutionary implication, with Sasha's odd Dostoevsky-quoting friend who seems more like a co-conspirator than a fellow invalid, and Sasha's farewell to Nadya in which he congratulates her on her decision and speaks of the possible "sacrifice" for which "our grandchildren and great-children will thank you."

In the spring of 1904, a few months after the gala opening of *The Cherry Orchard* in Moscow, Chekhov's doctor ordered him abroad to the German spa of Badenweiler, where (planning to go to Italy, "whither I am drawn irresistibly") he died on July 3rd.

Shortly after the news was received the newspaper *Russ'* (*Russia*) sent a special correspondent to Yasnaya Polyana to take down verbatim a few words from Tolstoy on Chekhov's death. Though not always agreeing with him, Chekhov had always revered Tolstoy who, he once wrote to a relative in Taganrog, "is Celebrity No. 1 in St. Petersburg and Moscow, I am Celebrity No. 877." Writing to his friend Mikhail Menshikov early in 1900, when he was sick himself but far more worried about reports of Tolstoy's illness, he said: "I never loved any man as I love him . . . while there is a Tolstoy in literature it is pleasant and agreeable to be a writer . . . Without him we should have been a shepherdless flock." Now that great man, who in Chekhov's lifetime had sometimes seemed to underestimate him, rose to the occasion with his usual simplicity and force. His impromptu epitaph, remarkable for its generosity and foresight, shows his full realization of Chekhov's importance and his place in literature. We give Tolstoy's words below, as they appeared in number 212, *Russia*, 15 July 1904.[1]

[1] This newspaper item, quoted in the magazine *Russkaya Literatura* (*Russian Literature*), Leningrad, no. 2, 1962, did not appear in the full Collected Works of L. N. Tolstoy (Jubilee edition).

Introduction

After a tribute to Chekhov as "an incomparable artist," and to his universal appeal, Lev Nikolaivich went on: "But this is the main thing . . . He was unreservedly candid, and that is a great quality; he wrote about what he saw and how he saw it . . . And because of that unreserved candor he created new, to my mind completely new, forms of writing for the whole world, the like of which I have never met anywhere! His language is an unusual language. I remember when I first began to read him he struck me as strange and 'awkward,' but as I read him more and more this language captivated me . . . Yes, it was particularly captivating just because of this 'awkwardness,' or whatever I should call it, as though without any effort on your part he had implanted the most beautiful artistic images in your soul . . . I repeat, Chekhov created new forms and, setting aside all false modesty, I contend that in technique he, Chekhov, was far above me! . . . He was a writer unique of his kind . . . And I also want to tell you that Chekhov has another great merit: he is one of those rare writers, like Dickens and Pushkin and a few like them, who can be read and re-read many times—I know this from my own experience . . . And I can tell you—Chekhov's death is a great loss for us, the more so because as well as an incomparable artist, we have lost in him a charming, sincere and honorable man . . . This was a fascinating, modest, sweet man!"

Late-Blooming Flowers

[1882]

On a certain dark autumnal afternoon something was happening at the house of the Princes Priklonsky.

The old princess and her daughter, Princess Marusya, were standing in the young prince's room, wringing their hands and pleading with him. They were pleading as only unhappy, weeping women can: in the name of the Lord Jesus Christ, their honor and his father's ashes.

The old princess stood in front of him, motionless and weeping. After giving full rein to her tears and speeches, interrupting Marusya at every word, she hurled reproaches, harsh words and even oaths at the prince, and endearments and entreaties, too. . . . A thousand times she reminded him of the merchant Furov who had presented their promissory note for payment, of his late father who must now be turning over in his grave, and so on. She even reminded him of Dr. Toporkov.

Dr. Toporkov was a thorn in the flesh of the Priklonskys. His father had been the serf Senka, the late prince's valet. Nikifor, his maternal uncle, was to this day valet to Prince Yegorushka. And in his early childhood this same Dr. Toporkov would be slapped when he did a poor cleaning job on the princely knives, forks, boots or samovars. And now—isn't it laughable?—the young, brilliant doctor lives like a lord in an awfully big house and drives about in a carriage-and-pair as if to spite the Priklonskys, who go on foot and haggle endlessly whenever they do hire a carriage.

"He's respected by everyone," said the old princess, weeping and not drying her tears. "Everyone likes him; he is rich, handsome, accepted everywhere. . . . And he was your own former servant, Nikifor's nephew! I'm ashamed to say it. And why? Because he behaves himself well, doesn't go carousing about, nor keeping company with bad people . . . works from morning till night . . . And you? Oh, my God!"

Princess Marusya, a girl of twenty, pretty, like the heroine of an English novel, with wonderful flaxen ringlets and large intelligent eyes the color of the southern sky, was pleading with her brother Yegorushka with no less energy.

She spoke at the same time as her mother, and kissed her brother on his prickly mustache which smelt of sour wine, and stroked his bald patch and his cheeks and clung to him like a frightened puppy. She used none but tender words. The young princess could not say anything even faintly resembling a caustic re-mark to her brother. She loved him so much! In her opinion, her debauchee brother, the retired hussar Prince Yegorushka, was the personification of the highest truth and a model of the noblest virtues! She was convinced to the point of fanaticism that this drunken sot had a heart which all the good fairies of elfland might envy. She saw in him an unfortunate, misunderstood, unrecognized man. His drunken de-bauchery she excused almost with delight. Of course! Yegorushka had long ago convinced her that he drank out of grief, that in wine and vodka he was drowning a hopeless love which was consuming his soul, and that in the arms of lewd women he was trying to erase *her* lovely image from his cavalryman's head. And what kind of Marusya, what kind of woman, does not con-sider love a reason for anything, an excuse for every-thing? What kind indeed?

"*Georges!*" Marusya was saying, clinging to him and kissing his red-nosed haggard face. "You are drinking because of your grief, it's true . . . But if that's the case, forget about your grief! Do all unhappy people have to drink? Bear up, be brave, put up a fight! Be a Hercules! With such a mind as yours, with such an honorable, loving soul, one can endure the blows of fate. Oh, you unlucky failures, you are all cow-ards! . . ."

And Marusya (forgive her, reader) remembered

Turgenev's Rudin,* and proceeded to talk about him to Yegorushka.

Prince Yegorushka was lying on his bed, gazing at the ceiling with his tiny bloodshot eyes. There was a slight noise in his head and a pleasant fullness in the region of his stomach. He had just dined, drunk a bottle of red wine and now, smoking a three-kopeck cigar, was enjoying his rest. The most varied emotions and thoughts swarmed through his foggy brain and wretched little soul. He was sorry for his weeping mother and sister, and at the same time he wanted very badly to get them out of his room; they were hindering him from taking a nap and snoring in peace. He was angry because they dared lecture him, but at the same time he was tormented by little pangs of what was probably also a very little conscience. He was stupid—but not so stupid that he could not realize that the house of the Priklonskys was indeed on its last legs, thanks partly to him.

The princess and Marusya pleaded for a very long time. Lamps were lit in the drawing room, and some woman dropped in to visit them, but they kept up their pleading. In the end Yegorushka grew tired of tossing about, unable to sleep. He stretched himself noisily and said:

* Hero of Turgenev's famous early novel of the same name; a liberal sympathizer who, after years of ineffective discussion and theorizing, finally left Russia in disgust and died in Paris on the barricades.

[6]

"All right, I'll turn over a new leaf."

"On your word of honor as a gentleman?"

"May God punish me if I don't!"

His mother and sister clutched his hands and made him swear once more on his honor. Yegorushka swore again and said that lightning might strike him dead in this very place if he did not stop leading such a disorderly life. The old princess made him kiss the icon. He kissed it and crossed himself three times. In short, the oath given was the most genuine imaginable.

"We believe you!" said the princess and Marusya and rushed to embrace Yegorushka. They did believe him. Who could refuse to believe a word of honor, a desperate oath and the kissing of the icon, all taken together? And besides, where there is love there is reckless faith. Their spirits revived, the two of them, radiant like the Israelites of old celebrating the new Jerusalem, went forth to celebrate the new Yegorushka. Having sent their guest packing, they sat down in a corner and began whispering together about how their Yegorushka would reform and begin leading a new life . . . They made up their minds that Yegorushka would go far, that he would quickly improve their circumstances and that they would not have to suffer the extreme of poverty—that horrid Rubicon, the crossing of which must be endured by all spendthrifts. They even decided that Yegorushka would without fail marry a rich woman, and a beauty, too. He was so handsome, so clever and so distinguished that there could hardly be a woman who could help falling in love with him! And in conclusion the old princess recounted the stories of those ancestors whom Yegorushka would soon begin to emulate. Grandfather Priklonsky had been an ambassador and had spoken all European languages, his father had commanded one of the most famous regiments, and the son would become—would become—what would he become?

"Now you'll see what he'll become!" the young princess decided. "Now you'll see!"

Having put one another to bed, they continued to talk for a long time about the glorious future. The dreams they dreamed as they were falling asleep were most enchanting—so bright, that in their sleep they smiled from happiness. These dreams in all probability were fate's reward for the horrors they were to suffer on the following day. Fate is not always miserly; sometimes she even pays in advance.

About three in the morning, precisely at the time when the old princess was dreaming of her *bébé* in a general's magnificent uniform and Marusya in her sleep was applauding her brother for a brilliant speech he had just made, a plain Russian droshky drew up to the home of the Princes Priklonsky. In the droshky sat a waiter from the *Château des Fleurs* cabaret, holding in his arms the aristocratic body of Prince Yegorushka, dead drunk. Yegorushka was completely insensible, and dangled from the "wai'er's" arms like a slaughtered goose on its way to the kitchen. The driver jumped down from the box and rang the bell at the front door. Nikifor and the cook came out, paid off the driver, and the two men carried the drunken body upstairs. Old Nikifor, neither surprised nor horrified, undressed the numb body with practiced hands, laid it comfortably in the featherbed and covered it with a blanket. The servants uttered not a single word. They had long since grown used to treating their master as something that required carrying in, undressing and covering up, and consequently they were not in the least surprised or horrified. A drunken Yegorushka was for them the norm.

Next morning matters became alarming.

At about eleven o'clock, when the princess and Marusya were drinking their coffee, Nikifor came into the dining room and reported to Their Ladyships that there was something wrong with Prince Yegorushka.

"It looks like he's dying!" said Nikifor. "Please come and take a look at him!"

The faces of the princess and Marusya became white as a sheet. A little piece of biscuit fell from the princess's mouth. Marusya upset her cup and pressed both hands to her breast in which her anxious heart, taken by surprise, began to beat nervously.

"Well, he got home at three this morning, pretty

tight," said Nikifor in a quavering voice. "Nothing unusual. But now, God knows what's up with him; he's tossing and groaning . . ."

The princess and Marusya caught hold of one another and ran to Yegorushka's bedroom.

Yegorushka, greenish-white, disheveled and terribly thin, was lying under a heavy flannel blanket; he was breathing heavily, shivering and tossing from side to side. Neither his head nor his hands remained still for a moment, they were continually twitching and shaking. Groans were torn from his breast. On his mustache was visible a little fleck of something red, apparently blood. If Marusya had bent down and looked into his face she would have noticed a little cut on his upper lip and the absence of two teeth in his upper jaw. His whole body exuded heat and a smell of alcohol.

The princess and Marusya sank to their knees and began to sob.

"It is we who are guilty of his death!" cried Marusya, clutching her head. "We hurt him yesterday with our reproaches and . . . and he couldn't bear it! His heart is so tender! We are guilty, *maman!*"

And conscious of their guilt they both opened their eyes wide and clung together, trembling all over, just as people tremble and cling together when they see the roof about to cave in with a loud and horrible crack and crush them under its weight.

The cook was smart enough to run for a doctor. One arrived, Ivan Adolfovich, a tiny little man, largely made up of a very big bald spot, foolish piggy eyes and a small round paunch. They were as glad to see him as if he had been their own father. He sniffed the air in Yegorushka's bedroom, felt his pulse, took a deep breath and made a wry face.

"Be not alarmed, Your Highness!" said he to the old princess in a pleading voice. "I know not, but to mine opinion, Your Highness, I find not your son is in great, so to say, danger . . . It is nudding."

To Marusya, however, he said something quite different.

"I know not, Prinzess, but to mine opinion . . . Everyone has his opinion, Prinzess. To *mine* opinion, his highness—pff! *Schwach,* as we Germans say . . . But it all depends . . . it depends, so to say, from the crisis."

"Is it dangerous?" Marusya asked softly.

Ivan Adolfovich knitted his brows and began explaining that everyone has his own opinion . . . They gave him a three-ruble note. He thanked them, became embarrassed, coughed and vanished into thin air.

Coming to their senses, the princess and Marusya decided to send for the "celebrity." Celebrities are expensive, but . . . what is one to do? The life of a dear one is more precious than money. The cook ran to fetch Toporkov. Of course he did not find the doctor at home, and had to leave a note. Toporkov did not hurry to answer the invitation. They waited for him all day, anxiously, with sinking hearts; they waited all night; all next morning. . . . They were even thinking of sending for another doctor and had made up their minds to call Toporkov a boor right to his face when he arrived, so that another time he would not make others wait so long for him. The inhabitants of the house of the Princes Priklonsky despite their grief were outraged to the depths of their souls. At last, at two o'clock on the second afternoon, a carriage drove up to the portico. Nikifor hurried with his mincing steps to the door and a few seconds later was with the utmost deference removing the broadcloth greatcoat from his nephew's shoulders. Toporkov announced his arrival with a cough and without greeting anyone set out for the patient's room. He passed through the hall, the drawing room and the dining room without looking at anyone, imperiously, with the air of a general, the whole house squeaking under his gleaming boots. His massive figure commanded respect. He was stately, pompous, impressive, with strikingly regular features, as if carved out of ivory. His gold-rimmed spectacles and immobile, extremely stern face added to his haughty bearing. He was a plebeian by origin, but almost nothing of the plebeian remained in him except his strongly developed muscles. Everything about him was aristocratic, even "gentlemanly." His face was ruddy, handsome, and even—if one is to believe his female patients—very handsome. His neck was as white as a woman's. His hair was soft as silk and beautiful but, regrettably, cropped short. Had Toporkov been interested in his appearance he would not have cut his hair, but allowed it to fall in waves to his very collar. His face was handsome, but too dry and grave to seem pleasant. Dry, grave and immobile, it expressed nothing except the extreme fatigue of a hard, full day's work.

Marusya went to meet Toporkov and, wringing her hands in front of him, began to plead with him. Never had she done such a thing before, with anyone.

"Save him, Doctor!" she said, raising her large eyes to him. "I implore you! You are our only hope!"

Toporkov walked round her and set off for Yegorushka's room.

"Open the window vents!" he ordered, going into the patient's room. "Why aren't the vents open? How can anyone breathe?"

The princess, Marusya and Nikifor rushed to the windows and the stove. The double windows, already fixed for winter, turned out to have no vents. The stove had not been lit.

"There are no vents in the windows," said the old princess timidly.

"That's strange . . . Mmmmm . . . How can I

[*13*]

treat sick people under these conditions! I won't do it!"

And slightly raising his voice Toporkov added:

"Move him into the hall. It's not so stifling there. Call the servants!"

Nikifor hurried to the bed and stood at the head of it. The princess, blushing—because except for Nikifor, the cook and a half-blind housemaid she had no other servants—grasped the bed. Marusya, too, took hold of it and pulled with all her might. The decrepit old man and the two feeble women lifted the bed with groans and, not trusting their own strength, stumbling and afraid of dropping it, carried it out. The old princess's dress ripped across her shoulders and something tore in her stomach; everything turned green before Marusya's eyes and her arms hurt dreadfully—Yegorushka was so heavy. But he, Toporkov, Doctor of Medicine, strode importantly along behind the bed and frowned angrily because they were taking up his time with such trifles. And he did not even lift a finger to help the ladies! What a brute!

They set the bed beside the grand piano. Toporkov removed the blanket and began undressing the tossing Yegorushka while asking the princess questions. Yegorushka's shirt was off in one second.

"Make it shorter, please! This is beside the point!" rapped out Toporkov as he listened to the princess. "Everyone who isn't needed may get out!"

Having tapped Yegorushka's chest with his mallet,

he turned the sick man over on his stomach and tapped again; he listened, puffing softly—doctors always puff softly while they listen—and diagnosed a drunken fever without complications.

"It won't hurt to put a straitjacket on him," said he, rapping out each word in his level voice.

Having given a few more instructions, he wrote out a prescription and marched rapidly to the door. While writing the prescription he had asked among other things for Yegorushka's family name.

"Prince Priklonsky," said the princess.

"Priklonsky?" repeated Toporkov.

How quickly you have forgotten the name of your former . . . landlord, thought the princess. She could not bring herself to think of the word "masters." The figure of the former serf was too awe-inspiring!

She approached him in the entrance hall and asked with a beating heart, "Doctor, he isn't in danger, is he?"

"I don't think so."

"Do you think he will recover?"

"I dare say," replied the doctor coldly, and with a slight nod of his head he went down the stairs to his horses, which were just as stately and impressive as he himself.

After the doctor had left, the princess and Marusya breathed easily for the first time in twenty-four anxious hours. The celebrity Toporkov had given them hope.

"How considerate, how nice he is!" said the princess, blessing in her heart all the doctors in the world. Mothers love Medicine and believe in it when their children are sick!

"An imp-o-o-o-o-rtant gentleman!" Nikifor remarked, having seen no one but Yegorushka's good-for-nothing drunken friends at his master's house for a long time. The poor old man never dreamt that this important gentleman was none other than his own grubby Kol'ka, the very same whom in days gone by he had often dragged by the heels from under the water cart and flogged.

The princess concealed from him that the doctor was his nephew.

That evening after sunset Marusya, exhausted from grief and fatigue, was overtaken by a violent chill which forced her into bed. The chill was followed by a raging fever and a pain in her side. All night long she lay delirious and groaned, "I'm dying, *maman!*"

And Toporkov, arriving at ten o'clock next morning, had to treat two instead of one—Prince Yegorushka and Marusya. He found Marusya had pneumonia.

The house of the Priklonskys began to smell of death. Invisible but terrible, death appeared at the head of both beds, threatening to steal the old princess's children from her at any moment. The princess was mad with despair.

"I don't know," Toporkov would say to her. "I can't

tell, I'm not a prophet. It will be clear in a few days."

He spoke these words dryly, coldly, and cut the old woman to the heart. Oh, for a single word of hope! To complete her misery Toporkov prescribed almost nothing for the invalids but spent his time only tapping and listening and scolding because the air was not fresh and the compress not applied at the right place or in time. The old lady regarded all these newfangled details as nonsensical and useless. Day and night, never stopping, she roamed from one bed to the other, forgetting everything else in the world, making vows and praying.

She thought of fever and pneumonia as really fatal illnesses, and when Marusya began to spit blood she imagined that the young princess was in "the last stages of consumption," and fainted away.

Imagine her joy when on the seventh day of her illness the young princess smiled and said,

"I'm well again."

On the seventh day Yegorushka, too, came round. With the adoration due to a demigod, the old princess, laughing and crying from happiness, went up to Toporkov on his arrival and said to him,

"I owe my children's lives to you, Doctor. *Thank* you!"

"What is it?"

"I owe you so much! You have saved my children!"

"Ah . . . The seventh day! I expected it on the

fifth. However, it makes no difference. Give them this powder morning and evening. Continue with the compresses. You can change his heavy blanket for a lighter one. Give your son something acid to drink. I will drop in again tomorrow."

And the famous man, with a parting nod of his head, strode back toward the staircase at his measured general's pace.

A clear, translucent, slightly frosty day—one of those autumn days for which you gladly put up with the cold and the damp and the heavy rubber boots. The air is so clear you can see the beak of a jackdaw sitting on the highest steeple; everything is saturated with the smell of autumn. Go out into the street and your cheeks will glow with a healthy, high color, bringing to mind fine Crimean apples. Yellow leaves, fallen long ago, lie trampled underfoot, yellowing in the sunshine, flashing like gold pieces, patiently awaiting the first snow. Nature is quietly and peacefully falling asleep. Not a breath of wind, not a sound. Motionless and dumb, silent, as though wearied by spring and summer, she lies basking in the warm caressing rays of the sun, and as you gaze upon this first peacefulness, you feel at peace yourself. . . .

It was just such a day when Marusya and Yegorushka sat at the window, awaiting Toporkov for the last time. The light—warm and caressing—shone through the windows of the Priklonsky house; it played over the rugs, the chairs, the grand piano. Everything was flooded with this light. Marusya and Yegorushka were looking out of the window onto the street and rejoicing in their recovered health. Convalescents, especially if they are young, are always very happy. They feel and appreciate good health as the ordinary healthy person can neither feel nor appreciate it. Health is freedom, yet who except a freed serf takes pleasure in the consciousness of liberty? Marusya and Yegorushka were conscious each moment of the end of their serfdom. How wonderful they felt! They wanted to breathe, to look out of the window, to move about, in a word to live, and all these desires were fulfilled every second. All was forgotten now—Furov and his promissory notes, the gossip, Yegorushka's conduct, and their own poverty. The only things not forgotten were the pleasant ones, those that caused no disquiet: the fine weather, prospective balls, dear *maman* and . . . the doctor. Marusya laughed and talked incessantly. The main topic of her conversation was the doctor, whom they were expecting any minute.

"What a wonderful man, he can do anything!" she was saying. "How omnipotent is his knowledge! Judge for yourself, *Georges*, how great a feat: to fight against nature and overcome it!"

As she talked, her hands and eyes made a big exclamation point after each high-flown but sincerely spoken phrase.

Blinking and nodding, Yegorushka listened to his sister's enthusiastic words. He respected Toporkov's stern face, himself, and was certain that he owed his recovery to him alone. *Maman* sat nearby and radiantly and triumphantly joined in her children's raptures.

Toporkov delighted her not only with the skill of his treatment but with that "positive quality" which she had learned to read in the doctor's face. For some reason this "positive quality" appeals very strongly to old people.

"I'm only sorry that he . . . that he is of such low origin," said the princess, glancing shyly at her daughter. "And his profession—it's not particularly clean. He is always up to the elbows in all sorts of things . . . Phew!"

The young princess flushed and moved to another armchair, further from her mother. The words grated upon Yegorushka, too.

He had no patience with her lordly arrogance or these airs and graces.

But poverty will teach anyone, you see! He himself had had to suffer more than once from the airs and graces of people who were richer than he.

"Nowadays, *Mutter*," he said, shrugging his shoulders contemptuously, "whoever has a head on his shoulders and a big pocket in his trousers is of good origin, but whoever has his behind where his head should be, and a soap bubble instead of a pocket, well, he's just zero and that's all there is to it!"

In saying this, Yegorushka was acting the parrot. He had heard these same words two months ago from a certain seminarian with whom he had had a fight in a billiard room.

"I should be glad to exchange my title for his head and his pocket," added Yegorushka.

Marusya looked up at her brother, full of gratitude.

"I could say a great deal to you, *maman*, but you wouldn't understand," she sighed. "Nothing will change your mind. It's too bad!"

The princess, caught out as a reactionary, was embarrassed and attempted to justify herself.

"Still, I used to know a doctor at Petersburg. He was a baron," she said. "Yes, yes . . . and abroad too . . . It's true. Education means a great deal. Well, yes . . ."

Toporkov arrived at one o'clock. He came in exactly as he had the first time: walking importantly, looking at no one.

"Don't drink any strong liquor, and avoid all excess as far as possible," he said, turning to Yegorushka, having put down his hat. "Watch out for your liver. It's already considerably enlarged. The enlargement is due entirely to consumption of strong drink. Take only the prescribed mineral waters."

And turning to Marusya he gave her, too, a few final words of advice.

Marusya heard him out attentively, as though listening to an absorbing story, looking straight into the eyes of this learned man.

"Well? You did understand, I suppose?" Toporkov asked her.

"Oh yes! *Merci.*"

The visit had lasted exactly four minutes.

Toporkov coughed, picked up his hat and nodded. Marusya and Yegorushka fixed their eyes on their mother. Marusya even began to blush.

The princess, waddling like a duck and red-faced, approached the doctor and awkwardly pushed her hand into his white fist.

"Please let us show our gratitude!" she said.

Yegorushka and Marusya dropped their eyes. Toporkov raised his closed hand toward his spectacles and perceived the roll of bills. Neither abashed nor lowering his eyes, he moistened his finger in his mouth and almost inaudibly counted the banknotes. He counted twelve 25-ruble notes. Not for nothing had Nikifor run to a certain place yesterday with his mistress's bracelets and earrings! A bright glow lit up Toporkov's face, something like the radiance with which holy men are depicted; a slight smile contorted his mouth.

Apparently he was very pleased with his fee. After counting the money and putting it in his pocket, he nodded once again and turned to the door.

The princess, Marusya and Yegorushka glued their eyes on the doctor's back, and all three of them simultaneously felt their hearts sinking. Their eyes glowed with warm emotion: this man was leaving and would never come again, but by now they had become accustomed to his measured step, his staccato voice and his serious face. A little notion suddenly flashed into the mother's head. All of a sudden she wanted very badly to show this wooden individual some kindness.

He is an orphan, poor boy, she thought. He is lonely.

"Doctor," said she, in a gentle, old woman's voice.

The doctor glanced back.

"What is it?"

"Won't you have a cup of coffee with us? Please be so kind!"

Toporkov frowned and slowly drew his watch from his pocket. He looked at the time, thought for a moment, and said:

"I will have some tea."

"Please sit down! Right here!"

Toporkov put down his hat and sat down; he sat straight, like a tailor's dummy with its knees bent into position and its head and shoulders straightened. The princess and Marusya bustled about. Marusya's eyes

[23]

grew enormous and worried, as though she were faced with an insoluble problem. Nikifor, wearing a worn black cutaway coat and gray gloves, ran in and out of all the rooms. Every corner of the house resounded with the noise of tea-things and the tinkling of tea-spoons. Yegorushka was for some reason called out of the hall for a minute, quietly and mysteriously.

Toporkov sat still for about ten minutes waiting for his tea. He sat and looked at the pedals of the piano, not moving a limb and not making a sound. At last the door from the drawing room opened. A beaming Nikifor appeared with a big tray in his hands. On the tray were two glasses in silver holders: one for the doctor, the other for Yegorushka. Around the glasses, in a strict symmetry, stood small pitchers of light and heavy cream, sugar and tongs, circles of lemon with a little fork, and biscuits.

Behind Nikifor came Yegorushka, his face a lifeless mask of self-importance.

The princess, her forehead damp with perspiration, and Marusya, very wide-eyed, brought up the rear of the procession.

"Do have some tea, please!" the princess invited Toporkov.

Yegorushka took a glass, walked to one side and carefully took a sip. Toporkov took a glass and also sipped. The princess and her daughter sat some distance away and occupied themselves with studying the doctor's face.

"Perhaps it's not sweet enough for you?" inquired the princess.

"No, it's sweet enough."

And, as one might have expected, a silence ensued—awful, horrible, the kind when for some reason one feels extremely awkward and inclined to retire into oneself. The doctor drank and said nothing. Seemingly he was unconscious of those around him and saw nothing in front of him except his tea.

The princess and Marusya, who wanted terribly to talk to this clever man, did not know what to begin with; they were both afraid of appearing foolish. Yegorushka watched the doctor and from the look in his eyes it was obvious that he meant to ask something but could in no way manage it. A sepulchral silence fell, broken now and again by sounds of swallowing. Toporkov swallowed very loudly. Apparently he was not shy about it, and drank as he felt like doing. In swallowing his tea he made noises much resembling the sound 'glee.' Each swallow seemed to drop from the inside of his mouth down a kind of precipice and there splashed against some large smooth object. Nikifor too broke the silence from time to time; every now and then he champed his lips and chewed a little, as though trying the taste of the doctor-guest.

"Is it true that smoking is harmful?" Yegorushka at last brought out.

"Nicotine, an alkaloid of tobacco, acts on the organism like one of the strong poisons. The poison, which enters the organism through each cigarette, is insignificant in amount, but its introduction is of long duration. The amount of the poison, like its strength, is in inverse proportion to the duration of its consumption."

The princess and Marusya exchanged glances. What a brilliant man! Yegorushka blinked and screwed up his fishlike face. Poor fellow, he had not understood the doctor.

"We had an officer in our regiment," he said, wishing to turn this learned conversation towards the commonplace. "A certain Koshechkin, a very decent fellow. Awfully like you! Awfully! As alike as two drops of water. It would be impossible to tell you apart. Isn't he a relative of yours?"

Instead of an answer the doctor made a loud swallowing noise, and the corners of his mouth lifted slightly in a wry, scornful smile. He plainly despised Yegorushka.

"Tell me, Doctor, am I really absolutely well now?" asked Marusya. "May I count on a full recovery?"

"I dare say. I am counting on a complete recovery on the basis of . . ."

And the doctor, holding his head erect and looking

straight at Marusya, began explaining the aftereffects of pneumonia. He spoke in his measured way, pronouncing each word distinctly, neither raising nor lowering his voice. They listened to him more than readily and with delight, but unfortunately this dry man could not popularize, nor did he consider it necessary to garble the facts a little to fit in with other people's way of thinking. Several times he used words like 'abscess,' 'coagulated regeneration,' and in general spoke very well and beautifully, but very unintelligibly. He went through a whole lecture, interlarded with medical terms without using a single phrase which his listeners could understand. However, this did not prevent them from sitting openmouthed and gazing at the learned man almost with veneration. Marusya could not tear her eyes away from his lips and hung on his every word. She gazed upon him and compared his face with those she was used to seeing every day.

How unlike this wise, tired face were the vacant, haggard faces of her suitors, Yegorushka's friends, who plagued her every day with their visits. The faces of the vicious and debauched—from whom she, Marusya, had never heard a single good, decent word—could not hold a candle to this cold and impassive, but intelligent and haughty face.

What a fascinating face! thought Marusya, enraptured by his face, and his voice and his words.

What a mind, and how much he knows! Why is *Georges* a soldier? He ought to be a scholar, too.

Yegorushka looked fondly at the doctor and thought: If he is talking about intellectual matters, then that means he considers us intellectual, too. It's fine that we should be considered so in society. What an awful fool I made of myself, lying to him about Koshechkin.

When the doctor had finished his lecture, his listeners drew a deep breath, as though they had just accomplished some kind of glorious exploit.

"How wonderful to know everything!" sighed the old princess.

Marusya got up and, as if desiring to express her gratitude to the doctor for his lecture, sat down at the piano and struck the keys. She wanted very much to draw him into a conversation, a deeper and more sentimental one, and music always induces conversation. And, too, she wanted to show off her talent before this brilliant, understanding man.

"This is from Chopin," said the old princess, smiling languidly and clasping her hands in her lap like an aristocratic schoolgirl. "What a charming thing! This girl of mine, Doctor . . . I must brag a little . . . is a beautiful singer too. She is my pupil . . . In days gone by I possessed a splendid voice. And now this ——" . . . the princess mentioned the name of a famous Russian singer . . . "You know her? She owes a great deal to me. Yes. I gave her lessons. She was a darling girl! Distantly related to my late husband, the prince . . . Do you enjoy listening to songs? But why do I ask? Who doesn't enjoy singing?"

Marusya began to play the best part of the waltz and looked around, smiling. She had to read on the doctor's face what impression her playing had made on him.

But she could not read anything at all. His face was just as emotionless and dry as before . . . He was quickly finishing his tea.

"I adore this part," said Marusya.

"Thank you," said the doctor. "I don't want any more."

He swallowed for the last time, got up and picked up his hat, expressing not the slightest desire to hear the waltz to the end. The old princess sprang up. Marusya, embarrassed and hurt, began to close the piano.

"You are going already?" said the old princess, frowning severely. "Would you like anything more? I hope, Doctor . . . You know the way now. Some evening perhaps . . . Don't forget us . . ."

The doctor nodded twice, awkwardly shook the hand the young princess held out to him and went silently out to get his fur coat.

"What an iceberg! What a stick!" said the princess, after the doctor's departure. "It's frightful! He can't smile, he's such a wooden statue! It was pointless playing for him, *Marie*! It's just as though he stayed only for the tea! He just drank and left!"

"But how intelligent he is, *maman*, so very intelligent! Who is there he could talk to in our house? I'm an ignoramus, *Georges* is secretive and never says a word . . . Can we really keep up an intelligent conversation? No!"

"Now there's a plebeian for you! There's Nikifor's nephew for you!" said Yegorushka, drinking up the cream in the pitchers. "And what a character! 'Rational, indifferent, subjective,'—how he spouts, the wretch! How do you like this plebeian? And what a carriage! Look! What swank!"

And all three of them looked out of the window at the carriage just as the famous man in his great bearskin coat was sitting down. The princess was green with envy and Yegorushka winked significantly and whistled. Marusya did not even see the carriage. She was too occupied to look at it, for she was scrutinizing the doctor who had made such an overpowering impression on her. Who is not affected by novelty?

But Toporkov was too new for Marusya.

The first snow fell, followed by the second and the third, and winter closed in for a long stay with its crackling frosts, snowdrifts and icicles. I don't like the winter and I don't believe the person who claims he does. Cold in the street, smoky in the house, wet in one's galoshes. Now harsh like a mother-in-law, now whining like an old maid, for all its enchanting moonight nights, troikas, hunts, concerts and balls, winter very quickly becomes a bore, and it stretches on too long, poisoning more than one homeless consumptive life.

In the home of the Princes Priklonsky life ran on in its customary way. Yegorushka and Marusya were now quite well and even their mother had stopped regarding them as invalids. Circumstances, as before, showed not the least sign of improving. Matters became ever worse and worse, money ever scarcer and scarcer. The princess pawned and pawned again all her jewels, inherited and acquired. Nikifor, as before, chattered in the grocery store where they sent him to get various small items on credit, that his masters owed him three hundred rubles and had no intention of paying him. And the cook, to whom the storekeeper, out of compassion had made a present of his old boots, chattered in exactly the same way. Furov became still more pressing. He refused to accept any more delays and was impudent to the princess when she begged him to postpone presentation of their note. Following in Furov's footsteps, their other creditors also began to clamor. Every morning the princess had to receive notaries, bailiffs and creditors. It seemed an auction for bankruptcy was being prepared.

The princess's pillow was as usual never dry from her tears. By day the princess stood firm, but at night she gave full vent to her tears and wept the whole night through. It wasn't necessary to look far for the reason. The reasons were under one's very nose; they struck the eye in sharp and brilliant relief. Poverty, self-respect incessantly outraged, . . . and by whom? By wretched little people like Furov, cooks, petty tradesmen. Her beloved possessions had gone into pawn, and parting with them cut the princess to the very heart. Yegorushka, as before, led a disorderly life, Marusya was still unattached . . . was all this not cause enough for weeping? The future was obscure, but through the fog the princess could perceive ominous specters. There was little hope for this future; nothing to be hoped for from it, much to be feared . . .

Money was scarcer and scarcer all the time, but Yegorushka indulged himself more and more, urgently, desperately, as though he wanted to make up for time lost during his illness. He spent everything on drink, both what he had and what he did not have, his own and others' money. In his licentiousness he was as insolent and rude as the devil. To borrow money from the first comer didn't worry him at all. It was habitual with him to sit down to play cards without a penny in his pocket, and he considered it no sin to gorge on food and drink at another's expense or to go for a ride in a hired carriage without paying the driver. He had changed very little: earlier he had been angry when people laughed at him; now he was only slightly embarrassed when he was thrown out or otherwise forced to leave a place.

Only Marusya had changed. She had learnt something new, and the news was terrible. She began to be disillusioned by her brother. For some reason it suddenly appeared to her that he was nothing like an unappreciated, misunderstood man, but simply a very ordinary person, a man just like all the rest, only even worse . . . she'd stopped believing in his hopeless love. What terrible news! Sitting for hours by the window and staring aimlessly out into the street, she pictured to herself her brother's face and tried hard to read in it some grace which would quench her disillusion, but she did not succeed in reading anything in this lusterless face except: worthless creature! trash! Along with his face there flashed into her mind those of his comrades, their visitors, her mother's old cronies, her suitors, and the tearful grief-dulled face of the old princess herself—and Marusya's poor heart was wrung with sadness. How petty, empty and colorless, how stupid, boring and idle it was, being around such close and beloved, but utterly worthless people!

Her heart was wrung with sadness, and her soul was seized with a single, passionate, heretical desire . . . Sometimes there were moments when she longed passionately to go away, but where? To that place, of course, where people lived who did not tremble before poverty, did not lead depraved lives, but worked hard, did not pass their time chatting all day long with silly old women and drunken fools . . . And one decent, wise face stuck out like a nail in Marusya's imagination; she read intelligence, a tremendous knowledge and weariness into this face. It was impossible to forget this face. She saw it every day, and in the happiest circumstances—namely, when its owner was working, or gave the impression of working.

Every day Dr. Toporkov would flash by the Priklonsky house in his luxurious sleigh with its bearskin rug and its stout coachmen. He did indeed have a great many patients. He paid visits from early morning till late evening and managed during the day to cover every street and alley. He sat in the sleigh just as in an armchair, imposingly, holding his head and shoulders very straight, not looking to either side. Nothing could be seen above the soft collar of his bearskin coat except his white smooth forehead and his gold-rimmed spectacles, but to Marusya that was quite enough. It seemed to her that the eyes of this benefactor of humanity were emitting cold, proud and contemptuous rays through the spectacles.

This man has a right to be contemptuous! she thought. He is so wise! What a magnificent sleigh, though, what wonderful horses! And this a former serf! What giant strength one must possess to be born a lackey and climb to such forbidding heights as he has!

Marusya alone remembered the doctor, but the others were already beginning to forget about him and soon would have forgotten him altogether had he not reminded them of himself. He reminded them of himself altogether too poignantly.

On the day after Christmas, at noon, when the Priklonskys were at home, the outside bell rang timidly. Nikifor answered the door.

"Is the dear Princess at h-o-o-o-o-me?" came an old woman's voice from the hall, and a little old woman tottered into the drawing room without waiting for an answer. "How do you do, dear Princess, your Ladyship . . . my benefactress! How are you, if you please?"

"What do you want?" asked the princess, looking curiously at the old woman. Yegorushka burst out laughing behind his hand. It seemed to him that the old woman's head looked exactly like a little overripe melon, with the stalk upwards.

"Don't you recognize me, little mother? You really don't remember me? Have you forgotten Prokhorovna? It was me delivered the young prince!"

And the old woman shuffled up to Yegorushka and suddenly kissed his chest and his hand resoundingly.

"I can't understand it," muttered Yegorushka crossly, wiping his hands on his coattails. "That old devil Nikifor lets in all sorts of tra . . ."

"What do you want?" repeated the princess, and it seemed to her that a strong smell of lamp oil came from the old woman.

[35]

The old woman settled herself into an armchair and after an interminable preamble, smirking coquettishly —matchmakers are always coquettish—announced that the princess had something to sell and she, the old woman, had a purchaser. Marusya's face flamed. Yegorushka snorted but, his curiosity aroused, walked over to the old woman.

"That's odd," said the princess. "Does this mean you have come with a proposal of marriage? I congratulate you, *Marie*, on your suitor! And who is he? May we know?"

The old woman puffed and panted, reached into her bosom and pulled out a red calico kerchief. Untying the knots in the kerchief she shook it over the table and a small photograph fell out along with a thimble.

They all averted their noses; from the red kerchief with its yellow flowers came a powerful smell of tobacco.

The princess picked up the photograph and languidly held it up to her eyes.

"A handsome fellow, little mother," the matchmaker began, describing the picture. "He's rich, noble . . . A wonderful man, a teetotaler . . ."

The princess flushed and handed the photograph to Marusya. The girl turned pale.

"Strange," said the princess. "If the doctor so desires, I should think he himself could . . . Matchmaking is the last thing we need here! An educated man, and then all of a sudden . . . He *did* send you? Himself?"

"He himself. He likes you terribly . . . A good family."

Marusya suddenly gave a little scream and rushed headlong from the room, clutching the photograph in her hands.

"How odd," went on the princess. "Most surprising . . . I don't quite know what to say to you . . . I had never expected anything like this from the doctor . . . Why did you have to trouble yourself? He could surely have come himself . . . It's even insulting . . . What does he take us for? We aren't some kind of tradesmen. And even tradesmen have begun to live differently now."

"What a character!" muttered Yegorushka, looking with disdain at the old woman's small head.

The retired hussar would have given much to be permitted to 'take a crack' at that small head just once! He hated old women as a big dog hates cats, and he showed a dog's enthusiasm at the sight of that melonlike head.

"What about it, little mother?" said the matchmaker, breathing heavily. "Maybe he wasn't born a prince, but I can say, little mother-princess . . . You are all our benefactors, aren't you? Oh dear, oh dear! But isn't he noble in every way? He's had all sorts of education, and he's rich, and Holy Mother! the Lord has bestowed all kinds of luxury upon him . . . but if you'd like him to come and call on you, then please . . . he'd be delighted to. Why shouldn't he come? He can come . . ."

And, taking the princess by the shoulder, the old matchmaker pulled her close and whispered into her ear; "He's asking sixty thousand—it's the usual thing. A wife's a wife, but money's money. You know yourself . . . I can't marry without money, he says, because my wife must have every kind of comfort . . . so she should have her own capital . . ."

The princess turned scarlet and, rustling her heavy skirts, arose from her chair.

"Be good enough to inform the doctor that we are extremely surprised," she said. "Most offended. This is wrong. I can't say anything else to you. . . . Why don't you say something, *Georges?* Let her go! There's a limit to anyone's patience."

After the matchmaker had left, the princess clutched her head in both hands, fell onto the couch and moaned.

"Oh that we should live to see this!" she wailed. "My God! Some wretched quack, yesterday's lackey, making us a proposal! Noble! Ha, ha! What sort of nobility is that, may I ask? He sent *us* a matchmaker! Too bad your father is not here! He wouldn't have let this pass! Vulgar idiot! Boor!"

But the princess was not so much offended that a plebeian had asked for her daughter's hand, as that he had asked for sixty thousand rubles which she didn't have. The slightest allusion to her poverty was an outrage to her. She wailed till late in the evening and woke up twice in the night to cry again.

The matchmaker's visit made a greater impression on Marusya than on anyone else, however. The poor girl was thrown into a raging fever. Trembling all over she fell into bed, buried her burning head under the pillow and began to ask herself again and again as well as she was able, Can it be true?

The question was a puzzler. Marusya did not know how to answer it. It conveyed at the same time her amazement, her confusion and the secret joy that for some reason she was ashamed to confess and wanted to hide even from herself.

Can it be? He, Toporkov? . . . It can't be! Something's wrong. The old woman has things all mixed up.

And at the same time the most sweet, intimate and enchanting dreams, such as make the heart stand still and the head throb, swarmed through her brain, and an inexplicable happiness seized her whole little being. He, Toporkov, wanted to make her his wife, and look how graceful, how handsome, how clever he was! He had devoted his life to humanity and . . . he went about in such a magnificent sleigh!

Can it be true?

One could love him! Marusya concluded toward evening. Oh, I do consent! I am free from all prejudice and I will follow this serf to the end of the world! Just let mother say one word and I will leave her. I do consent!

The other questions, the secondary and even lesser ones, she had no time for. They were of no importance to her. What was the matchmaker doing here? Why and when had *he* fallen in love with *her*? Why had he not come himself, if he was in love? What concern had she with these and many other questions! She was surprised, astonished and overjoyed . . . and this was enough for her.

I do consent, she whispered, trying in her imagination to picture *his* face, with the gold-rimmed spectacles through which his wise, serious, tired eyes looked forth. Let him come! I do consent!

And while Marusya tossed on her bed in this manner and felt all her being on fire with happiness, the matchmaker was calling at shopkeepers' houses and scattering the doctor's photographs generously on all sides. Going from one rich man's house to another, she was looking for the goods for which she could recommend a "noble" purchaser. Toporkov had not sent her specifically to the Priklonskys. He had sent her 'wherever she wished.' On marriage itself, for which he felt the necessity, he looked quite indifferently: to him it was immaterial where the matchmaker called . . . He needed—sixty thousand. Sixty thousand, no less! The house he intended to buy could not be had for less than this sum. He could not borrow this amount anywhere, and they would not agree to instalment payments. There remained only one way out: to marry money, which he was now doing. Marusya, I assure you, was not in the least responsible for his desire to tie himself in Hymen's bonds.

At one o'clock that night Yegorushka came quietly into Marusya's room. Marusya was already undressed and trying to get to sleep. She was exhausted by her unexpected happiness; she wanted somehow to quiet her incessantly beating heart, which seemed to be beating through the whole house. In every wrinkle of Yegorushka's face there were a thousand secrets. He coughed mysteriously, glanced meaningfully toward Marusya and, as though wishing to impart to her something terribly important and secret, sat down on her feet and leaned down to her ear.

"You know what I'm going to say to you, Masha?" he began softly. "I will tell you frankly . . . My point of view is . . . Because I'm really thinking of your happiness. Are you asleep? I'm really thinking of your happiness. Marry him—this Toporkov! Don't make a fuss about it, marry him—and then . . .

that's it! He is the right sort of person in every way
. . . And he's rich. It doesn't mean a thing that he is
of low birth. A lot of rubbish!"

Marusya shut her eyes tight. She felt ashamed. And
at the same time she was very pleased that her brother
liked Toporkov.

"He's rich enough to make up for it! At least you
won't go without bread. But wait around for some
prince or count, and you'll probably end up dying of
hunger. We haven't even a kopeck! Pfft! All gone!
Are you asleep or what? Heh? Does your silence mean
consent?"

Marusya smiled. Yegorushka began to laugh and
for the first time in his life kissed her hand, very
warmly.

"Then go ahead and marry him . . . He's an educated man. And how wonderful it will be for us! The
old lady will stop howling!"

Yegorushka plunged into reverie. Having reflected
awhile, he shook his head and said, "There's only one
thing I don't understand . . . Why the devil did he
send this matchmaker? Why didn't he come himself?
There's something wrong here . . . He isn't the kind
of man to send a matchmaker."

That's true, thought Marusya, shuddering for some
reason. There *is* something wrong here . . . It was
stupid to send the matchmaker. Come to think of it,
what *does* it mean?

Yegorushka, who usually would not have had the sense to think the matter out at all, this time found an answer, "You know, though, he has no time to gad about himself. He's busy all day long. He dashes about like a madman calling on his patients."

Marusya relaxed, but not for long.

Yegorushka was silent for a little while, and then said, "And another thing seems odd to me: he told this old witch to say that the dowry should be not less than sixty thousand. Did you hear? Otherwise, he says, it's out of the question."

Marusya at once opened her eyes, her whole body trembled, and she sat up in bed forgetting even to cover her shoulders with the quilt. Her eyes sparkled and her cheeks flamed.

"Is that what the old woman says?" she said, tugging at Yegorushka's hand. "Tell her it's a lie! People like this—I mean people such as he—couldn't even say such a thing. He and . . . money? Ha ha! Only those who don't know how proud, how honest, how unmercenary he is could possibly have these low suspicions! Yes! He's a wonderful man! They just don't understand him!"

"I think so too . . ." said Yegorushka. "The old woman was lying. Maybe she wanted to worm herself into his favor. She has got this way from dealing with shopkeepers!"

Marusya nodded in agreement and hid her pretty

head under the pillow. Yegorushka stood up and stretched.

"Mother is howling," he said. "Well, we won't pay any attention to her. And so, what about it? Are you agreeable? Fine! Let's not give ourselves any airs. A doctor's wife—ha ha! A doctor's wife!"

Yegorushka patted Marusya on the sole of her foot and, very content, went out of the bedroom. As he was going to bed, he compiled in his head a long list of guests he intended to invite to the wedding.

We must get the champagne from Aboltukhov, he thought as he fell asleep. And hors d'oeuvres from Korchatov. His caviar is always fresh. And the lobsters, too . . .

Next morning Marusya, dressed simply but with taste and not without coquetry, sat down at the window and waited. At eleven o'clock Toporkov tore past, but he did not call. In the afternoon he once again hurried past with his jet-black horses under these very windows, but not only did he not call, he did not even glance up at the window near which Marusya was sitting with a pink ribbon in her hair.

He has no time, thought Marusya, looking at him adoringly. He will come on Sunday.

But he did not call on Sunday either. A month passed, and two, and three, and still he did not call. He was not thinking about the Priklonskys at all, of course, but Marusya waited and grew thin from waiting. Cats, not the ordinary kind but ones with long yellow claws, tore at her heart.

Why hasn't he come yet? she asked herself. Why? Oh yes, I know . . . He is hurt because . . . Why is he hurt? Because *maman* treated the old matchmaker so tactlessly. Now he thinks I can't possibly fall in love with him . . .

"B-b-beast!" muttered Yegorushka, who had called on Aboltukhov a dozen times and asked if he could get the very best champagne.

After Easter, which came at the end of March, Marusya stopped waiting.

Yegorushka came to her in her bedroom one day and, laughing spitefully, informed her that her 'fiance' had married a woman of the merchant class.

"I have the honor to congratulate you! I have the honor! Ha ha ha!"

This news was too cruel for my little heroine.

She lost heart altogether and not for a day or two but for months remained the embodiment of inexpressible grief and despair. She pulled the pink ribbon from her hair and began to hate her life. Yet how prejudiced and unjust emotion is! For even here Marusya found justification for *his* action. Not for nothing had she read so many novels in which people took a wife or a husband to spite those they loved, so that they would be made to understand, or be piqued, or sorely wounded.

[45]

He married this fool to spite me, thought Marusya. Oh, how wrong we were to dismiss his proposal so contemptuously! Such people don't forget insults!

The healthy color vanished from her cheeks, her lips forgot how to smile, her mind refused even to dream of the future—Marusya was distraught! It seemed to her that, with Toporkov lost, the meaning of life was lost for her, too. What good was her existence now, if there remained only idiots, parasites and drunkards to share it with! She fell into a deep depression. Paying attention to nothing, neither noticing nor hearing anything around her, she began to drag out her monotonous drab life as so many of our maiden ladies, old and young, have managed to do . . . She paid no attention to her suitors, of whom she had a great many, nor to her family or acquaintances. She looked upon her family's miserable circumstances indifferently, with apathy. She did not even care when the bank foreclosed on the house of the Princes Priklonsky, with all its historic possessions which had been so dear to her, nor when she had to move to new quarters, humble and cheap in the *petit-bourgeois* taste. She was in a long, heavy sleep, which nevertheless was not without its dreams. She dreamed of Toporkov in all his aspects: in his sleigh, in his furs, without his furs, sitting down, striding importantly along. This dream became her whole life.

But a thunderstorm broke . . . and the dream

vanished from the blue eyes with their flaxen lashes. The old princess, unable to endure their ruin, fell ill in the new lodgings and died, leaving her children nothing except her blessing and a few dresses. Her death was a terrible blow for the young princess. The dream vanished, to make way for sorrow in its place.

Autumn set in, as raw and muddy as last year's.

Outdoors, it was a gray, tearful morning. Dark gray clouds, as if smeared with mud, covered the entire sky, and their immobility produced the utmost gloom. It seemed the sun did not exist; it had not once looked down on the earth for a whole week, as though afraid of soiling its rays in the wet dirt.

The rain beat a tattoo on the windows with unusual force; the wind roared in the chimneys and howled like a dog that has lost its master . . . There was not a face to be seen in which one could not read a desperate boredom.

Better the most desperate boredom than the deep sadness reflected this morning on Marusya's face. Dragging herself through the wet mud, my heroine was plodding on her way to Dr. Toporkov's. Why was she going to him?

I am going for treatment! she thought to herself.

But do not believe her, reader! Not without cause can a struggle be read in her face.

The princess arrived at Toporkov's house and shyly,

with a palpitating heart, rang the bell. In a minute steps were heard behind the door. Marusya felt her legs freezing and buckling under her. The lock turned, and Marusya saw in front of her the inquiring face of a pretty housemaid.

"Is the doctor at home?"

"We aren't seeing people today. Tomorrow!" answered the maid and, shivering in the damp draft, she stepped back. The door slammed right in Marusya's face, shook slightly, and was noisily locked.

The young princess was disconcerted, and slowly made her way home. There she was met by a free spectacle, but one she had long ago tired of. It was far from princely.

Prince Yegorushka was sitting in the tiny living room, on a couch upholstered in shiny new calico. He sat Turkish fashion, with his legs crossed under him. Near him on the floor lay his good friend, Kaleriya Ivanovna. The two of them were playing cards "for noses" and drinking. The prince was drinking beer; his Dulcinea, madeira. The winner, together with the right to flick his opponent on the nose, also received a twenty-kopeck piece. A small concession was made to Kaleriya Ivanovna, as a lady: instead of twenty kopecks she was allowed to pay with a kiss. This game gave both of them inexpressible enjoyment. They rolled about with laughter, pinched each other, and at every other moment leapt out of their places and chased each other up and down. Yegorushka went into calflike raptures whenever he won. He was enchanted by the antics with which Kaleriya Ivanovna paid the kisses she lost.

Kaleriya Ivanovna, a long, thin brunette with terribly dark eyebrows and protuberant goggle eyes, came to see Yegorushka every day. She arrived at the Priklonskys' at ten o'clock in the morning, drank tea with them, had dinner and supper, and went home after midnight. Yegorushka assured his sister that Kaleriya Ivanovna was a singer, and a highly respectable lady, etc.

"You just talk to her," Yegorushka tried to persuade his sister. "She's a smart girl! Awfully smart!"

Nikifor, I think was more correct in calling Kaleriya Ivanovna 'Kavaleriya' * Ivanovna, and a tart too. He wholeheartedly despised her and was beside himself whenever he had to wait on her at the table. He sensed the truth, and the instinct of an old devoted servant told him that this woman had no place beside his masters . . . Kaleriya Ivanovna was stupid and frivolous, but that did not prevent her from leaving the Priklonskys every day with a full stomach, her winnings in her pocket, and the conviction that they could not live without her. She was the wife of the billiard marker at the club, that's all, but this did

* Russian for *cavalry*.

not prevent her from being absolute mistress in the Priklonsky house. This pig liked to put its feet on the table.

Marusya was living on a pension she had inherited from her father. It was larger than is usual for a general, but Marusya's share was insignificant; yet it would have been sufficient for a comfortable existence if only Yegorushka had not indulged so many whims.

Neither wanting nor knowing how to work, he did not wish to accept the fact that he was poor, and was very put out if anyone urged him to reconcile himself to his circumstances and moderate his whims as far as possible.

"Kaleriya Ivanovna doesn't like veal," he would often say to Marusya. "We must give her fried chicken. The devil take you! You set yourself up as a housekeeper, but you can't manage. Let's not have this rotten veal tomorrow! We'll starve the woman to death!"

Marusya contradicted him gently, but in order to avoid unpleasantness she would buy a young chicken.

"Why was there no roast today?" Yegorushka would yell sometimes.

"Because we had chicken yesterday," answered Marusya.

But Yegorushka knew very little about household arithmetic and did not wish to know anything. At dinner he persistently demanded beer for himself and wine for Kaleriya Ivanovna.

"How can one have a decent dinner without wine?" he demanded of Marusya, shrugging his shoulders in amazement at such stupidity. "Nikifor! We must have wine! It's your business to see to this! And you, Masha, ought to be ashamed! Don't make me take on the housekeeping myself. How you love to make me lose my temper!"

He was an unrestrained sybarite. Kaleriya Ivanovna soon came to his assistance.

"Is there wine for the prince?" she would ask when they sat down to dinner. "And where is the beer? Someone must go and get it! Princess, give the man the money for the beer! Have you some small change?"

The princess said yes, she had some small change, and handed over the last of it. Yegorushka and Kaleriya ate and drank and never noticed how Marusya's watches, rings and earrings were disappearing into pawn, piece by piece, and her expensive dresses passing to the old-clothesman.

They neither saw nor heard with what groans and mutterings old Nikifor would open his little trunk when Marusya borrowed money from him for tomorrow's dinner. To these trivial and obtuse people—the prince and his vulgar friend—all this mattered not at all.

On the next morning Marusya went to call on Toporkov at ten o'clock. The door was opened by the same pretty housemaid. Admitting the princess to the vestibule and helping her off with her coat, the maid drew in her breath and said, "I suppose you know, young lady, the doctor doesn't give a consultation for less than five rubles? You do know?"

Why does she speak to me this way? thought the princess. What insolence. He doesn't even know, poor man, that he has such an insolent servant!

And at the same time Marusya's heart skipped a beat: she had only three rubles in her pocket, but surely he wasn't going to drive her away for a miserable two rubles.

From the vestibule Marusya went into the waitingroom, where a great number of patients was sitting. The majority of those thirsting for healing were, of course, ladies. They occupied all the seats in the waitingroom and had settled themselves in groups for heart-to-heart talks. Extremely animated conversations were going on about everything and everybody: the weather, sicknesses, the doctor, children . . . They all spoke quite loudly and laughed boisterously, as though in their own homes. Some of the women knitted or embroidered while waiting their turn. There were no plainly or badly dressed people in the waitingroom. Toporkov received his patients in an adjoining room. They went in to him in turn. They went in with wan faces, serious, trembling slightly, but came out red and sweating, as they might have after confession, completely happy, as though released from some unbearable burden. Toporkov gave each patient not more than ten minutes. Their illnesses, evidently, were not serious.

All this is just so much charlatanism! It would have occurred to Marusya had she not been preoccupied with her own thoughts.

Marusya went into the doctor's consulting room last. As she entered this room, cluttered with books with German and French inscriptions on their covers, she shivered as a hen does when it is plunged into cold water. *He* was standing in the middle of the room, leaning his left hand on the desk.

How handsome he is! passed through his patient's head before anything else.

Toporkov did not consciously pose—he would hardly have known how to—but all the attitudes he ever assumed seemed on him particularly majestic. The pose in which Marusya had caught him now resembled the poses of those stately models from whom painters usually draw the great commanders. Near the hand he leaned on the desk were scattered the ten- and five-ruble notes he had just received from his women patients. Here, too, lay, in strict order, his instruments, forceps, test tubes—it was all extremely incomprehensible and extremely "scientific" to Marusya. All this and the office itself with its luxurious furnishings completed a majestic picture. Marusya closed the door behind her and stood still . . . Toporkov motioned her with his hand toward an armchair. My heroine went quietly to the chair and sat down. Toporkov swayed majestically, sat down in another chair opposite her and fixed his questioning eyes on Marusya's face.

He hasn't recognized me! thought Marusya. Otherwise he wouldn't keep silent. . . . Good Lord, why doesn't he say something? How on earth am I to begin?

"Well?" mumbled Toporkov.

"I have a cough," whispered Marusya and, as though in corroboration of her words, coughed twice.

"Have you had it long?"

"For about two months now . . . Mostly at night."

"Hmmm . . . any fever?"

"No, there doesn't seem to be any fever."

"It seems to me I have treated you before? What was the matter before?"

"Pneumonia."

"Hmmm . . . Yes, I remember. Your name is Priklonsky, I believe?"

"Yes . . . my brother was sick then, too."

"You will take this powder . . . before bedtime . . . avoid colds . . ."

Toporkov quickly wrote out a prescription, got up

and assumed his earlier pose. Marusya also stood up.

"Nothing further?"

"Nothing."

Toporkov fixed her with his eyes. He looked at her and at the door. He had no time to waste, and he was waiting for her to leave. But she stood and looked at him, lost in admiration and waiting for him to say something. How handsome he was! A minute passed in silence. At last she roused herself, noticed a yawn on his lips and expectation in his eyes, handed him three rubles and turned to the door. The doctor threw the money on the table and locked the door after her.

On the way home from the doctor's house, Marusya was terribly angry with herself.

Well, why didn't I speak to him? Why didn't I? Because I'm a coward, that's why! Everything turned out so stupidly . . . I only bothered him. Why ever did I hold that wretched money in my hand, as if to show off? Money . . . is such a delicate matter . . . God forbid! It's so easy to offend a man! One should pay somehow so as to do it inconspicuously. And then, why did I keep quiet? . . . He would have talked to me, explained things . . . I should have found out why the matchmaker came . . .

When she got home, Marusya lay down on her bed and hid her head under the pillow as she always did when she was upset. But she had no chance to calm herself. Yegorushka came into her room and began striding from corner to corner, his boots thumping and squeaking.

His face was mysterious . . .

"What do you want?" asked Marusya.

"I . . . er . . . I thought you were asleep, I didn't want to disturb you. I want to tell you something . . . something very nice. Kaleriya Ivanovna wants to come and live with us. I persuaded her."

"That's impossible! *C'est impossible! Whom* did you ask?"

"Why is it so impossible? She's a very nice girl . . . She'll help you with the housekeeping. We'll put her in the corner room."

"The corner room is where *maman* died! It's impossible!"

Marusya began to twitch and shake as though she had been stung. Red patches appeared in her cheeks.

"It's impossible! You will kill me, *Georges*, if you force me to live with this woman! Darling *Georges*, don't do it! My dearest, I *beg* you!"

"But why don't you like her? I don't understand! She is a woman like any other . . . intelligent, lively."

"I don't like her."

"Well, but I like her. I love this woman and I want her to live with me!"

Marusya began to sob . . . Her pale face was contorted with despair.

[56]

"I shall die if she comes to live here!"

Yegorushka began whistling something under his breath and, after walking back and forth a little while, left Marusya's room. In a moment he was back again.

"Lend me a ruble," he said.

Marusya gave him one. It was only right somehow to alleviate Yegorushka's distress at a time when, as she thought, a horrible struggle was going on within him, his love for Kaleriya fighting against his sense of duty!

Kaleriya came to the princess in the evening.

"Why don't you like me?" asked Kaleriya, throwing her arms round the princess. "If you only knew how unhappy I am!"

Marusya freed herself from her embrace and said, "There is no reason why I should like you."

She paid dearly for this remark. Kaleriya, having installed herself the following week in the room in which *maman* had died, found it necessary to revenge herself for this phrase first of all. She chose the crudest kind of revenge.

"Why do you put on such airs?" she would ask Marusya every dinnertime. "With such poverty as yours you shouldn't put on airs, but bow your head in front of decent people. If I had only known you had such faults, I wouldn't have come to live with you. And whatever did I fall in love with that brother of yours for?" she added with a sigh.

Reproaches, hints and smiles would end in loud

laughter at Marusya's poverty. This laughter was nothing to Yegorushka. He considered himself in Kaleriya's debt and held himself back. But the idiotic laughter of the billiard-marker's wife, Yegorushka's mistress, was poisoning Marusya's life.

Marusya spent whole evenings on end in the kitchen; helpless, weak, and irresolute, she would shed tears into Nikifor's broad palms. Nikifor would whimper with her and rub salt in her wounds with his recollections of the past.

"God will punish them!" he used to comfort her. "Don't you cry, now!"

In the winter Marusya went once again to Toporkov's.

When she entered his office, he was sitting in a chair, handsome and majestic as before . . . This time his face looked very tired . . . His eyes blinked like those of a man who has been prevented from getting his sleep. He motioned with his chin toward the armchair opposite him, not looking at Marusya. She sat down.

There is sadness in his face, thought Marusya, looking at him. Oh, he is probably very miserable with his tradeswoman!

They sat in silence for a minute. How delightful it would have been to complain to him of her life! She would have disclosed to him things such as could never be read in any of his books with their French and German inscriptions.

"I have a cough," she whispered.

The doctor glanced cursorily at her.

"Hmmm . . . Any fever?"

"Yes, in the evening."

"Do you perspire at night?"

"Yes."

"Undress."

"What do you mean?"

Toporkov made an impatient gesture towards his chest. Marusya, blushing, slowly unfastened the buttons over her breast.

"Get undressed. Be quick, please!" said Toporkov and took his mallet in his hand.

Marusya drew one hand out of her sleeve. Toporkov quickly went up to her and in the twinkling of an eye had pulled her dress down to her belt with his accustomed hand.

"Undo your chemise!" he said and, not waiting for Marusya to do it herself, unbuttoned her chemise at the neck and to the great horror of his patient began tapping with his mallet on her white, emaciated breast.

"Put your hands down . . . Don't get in my way. I won't eat you," muttered Toporkov, but she was blushing furiously and ardently wishing that the floor would open and swallow her up.

[59]

Having finished tapping, Toporkov began to listen. The sound at the top of the left lung seemed very dull. He could make out clearly a rasping rattle and hard dry breathing.

"Get dressed," said Toporkov and began asking her questions: Did she have good living quarters, was her daily regimen sound, etc.

"You must go away to Samara," he said, preaching her a whole sermon on the proper way of living. "You should drink kumiss* there. I've finished. You may go . . ."

Marusya fastened up her buttons somehow, awkwardly handed him five rubles and after waiting a moment went out of the office.

He kept me a full half-hour, she thought, going home. But I said nothing! Nothing! Why didn't I speak to him!

She went home, not giving a thought to Samara but thinking only of Dr. Toporkov. What did Samara mean to her? It was true there was no Kaleriya Ivanovna there, but on the other hand neither was there any Toporkov.

To blazes with it, this Samara! She walked along, angry and rejoicing at the same time. *He* had found her to be sick, and now she might visit him without

---

* Fermented mare's milk, believed to be valuable in the treatment of consumption. Chekhov himself in his later years often drank it.

ceremony as often as she liked, every week even! It was so wonderful in his consulting room, so cosy! Especially wonderful was the couch which stood in the depths of the room. She longed to sit with him awhile on this couch and talk over anything and everything, complain a little, advise him that he shouldn't charge his patients quite so much. Rich people, of course, should be charged a lot; but the poor, not so much.

He doesn't understand life, he can't tell the difference between rich and poor, thought Marusya. I would have taught him.

This time, too, another free spectacle awaited her at home. Yegorushka was tossing about on the couch in a fit of hysterics. He was sobbing, cursing, and shaking as though in a fever. Tears rolled down his drunken face.

"Kaleriya has gone!" he wailed. "She hasn't been home for two nights now! She got terribly angry!"

But Yegorushka was bellowing unnecessarily. In the evening Kaleriya returned, forgave him and drove away with him to the club.

Yegorushka's dissolute life had reached its apogee. Marusya's pension was not enough for him, so he began to 'work.' He borrowed money from the servants, cheated at cards, stole Marusya's money and belongings. One day, walking beside his sister, he filched two rubles from her pocket, which she had been saving to buy herself a pair of shoes. One ruble he kept for himself, and with the other he bought Kaleriya some pears. His companions left him. The former visitors to the Priklonsky home, Marusya's acquaintances, now addressed him to his face as "your Lordship the cardsharp." Even "the girls" of the *Château des Fleurs* eyed him distrustfully and laughed at him whenever, having borrowed money from some new acquaintance or other, he invited them to have supper with him.

Marusya saw and understood this climax of degradation.

Kaleriya's familiarity also mounted to a crescendo.

"Don't rummage about among my clothes, please," said Marusya to her one day.

"Nothing will happen to your clothes," answered Kaleriya. "But if you think I'm a thief, then . . . have it your way! I shall leave."

But Yegorushka, cursing his sister, groveled at Kaleriya's feet for a whole week, begging her not to leave.

Such an existence could not drag on for long. Every story comes to an end, and this little romance, too, came to its end.

Shrovetide began, and with it the days that are the heralds of spring. The days grew longer, rain poured from the roofs, and from the fields began to blow that fresh young wind by which one can sense that spring is near . . .

On one of these Shrovetide evenings Nikifor was sitting by Marusya's bed . . . Yegorushka and Kaleriya were not at home.

"I am terribly hot, Nikifor," said Marusya.

But Nikifor was sniveling and adding to her torments by his memories of the past . . . He spoke about the late prince and princess and about their former life . . . He described the forests where the late prince used to hunt, the fields across which he would chase the hares—and Sebastopol. (The late prince had been wounded at Sebastopol.) Nikifor told many stories. Marusya particularly liked his descriptions of the country estate which had been sold five years before to pay their debts.

"You'd go out there sometimes, onto the terrace . . . Spring was just beginning. And Lord! You couldn't tear your eyes away from God's earth! The forest was still dark, yet it was the very picture of joy. The little river was glorious, deep. . . . Your dear mother in her childhood used to go fishing with a rod and line . . . She'd stay by the water all day. She loved to be out of doors. Oh, Nature!"

Nikifor grew hoarse telling his stories. Marusya listened to him and would not let him go. On the old servant's face she could read everything he said about her father, her mother, the country place. She listened, peering closely into his face, and she felt a great longing to live, to be happy, to fish in that same river her mother had fished in . . . The river, the fields beyond the river, the forest a deep blue beyond the fields, and over all this the sun shining, tender and warm . . . How wonderful to be alive!

˙ "Nikifor, dearest," said Marusya, pressing his dry hand, "darling, lend me five rubles tomorrow . . . For the last time . . . will you?"

"I will . . . I only *have* five. Take them, and God will provide for us. . . ."

"I will pay you back, darling. Just lend them to me."

The next morning Marusya put on her best dress, tied her hair with a pink ribbon and went to call on Toporkov. Before leaving the house she glanced at herself a dozen times in the mirror. In Toporkov's vestibule a new maid met her.

"I suppose you know?" the new maid asked her, helping her off with her coat. "The doctor charges at least five rubles for a consultation. . . ."

On this occasion there was an exceptional number of women patients. All the chairs were taken. One man was even sitting on the piano. Reception of the patients began at ten. At twelve the doctor made a break for an operation, and began receiving again at two. Marusya's turn did not come until four o'clock.

Having had no tea, exhausted from waiting, shivering with fever and agitation, she did not notice how she came to be in the armchair facing the doctor. There was a sort of vacuum in her head, her mouth was dry, her eyes were misted over. Through this mist she could see nothing but things flashing before her eyes —*his* head, *his* hands, *his* mallet.

"Did you go to Samara?" the doctor asked. "Why didn't you go?"

She did not reply. He tapped her chest and listened. The dull sound on the left side had spread over almost the whole lung; it could be heard, too, at the top of the right lung.

"There is no need for you to go to Samara. Don't go," said Toporkov.

And Marusya, through the mist, read something slightly resembling compassion in his dry, serious face.

"I'm not going," she whispered.

"Tell your parents not to let you go out in the air. Avoid harsh, indigestible food . . ."

Toporkov began to give her advice, was carried away and read her a whole lecture.

She sat but heard nothing, and through the mist fixed her eyes on his moving lips. It seemed to her that he had been talking much too long. Finally he fell silent, stood up and, staring at her through his spectacles, waited for her to leave.

She did not go. She was happy to sit here in this fine armchair and it was dreadful to go home, to Kaleriya.

[65]

"That's all," said the doctor. "You may go."

She turned her face and glanced at him.

Don't drive me away! he would have read in her eyes if he had been even in the slightest degree a physiognomist.

Big tears splashed down, her arms fell feebly along the sides of her chair.

"I love you, Doctor!" she whispered.

And a red glow, resulting from an overpowering inner fire, spread over her face and neck.

"I love you!" she whispered once more. Her head swayed twice, sank down lifelessly, and her forehead touched the table.

And the doctor? The doctor . . . blushed for the first time in all the years of his practice. His eyes began blinking, like those of an urchin who has been ordered onto his knees for punishment. Never had he heard such words, and in such a form, from any of his woman patients! Nor from any woman at all! Had he heard aright?

His heart began to beat turbulently and knock against his side . . . He cleared his throat in embarrassment.

"Mikolasha!" a voice sounded from the adjoining room, and in the half-open door appeared the rosy cheeks of the shopkeeper's daughter he had married.

The doctor took advantage of this summons and

quickly left the office. He was glad to seize on anything at all to escape from the awkward situation.

When he returned to the room after ten minutes, Marusya was lying on the couch. She lay on her back with her face turned upward. One hand fell to the floor, together with a strand of her hair. She was unconscious. Toporkov, flushed, and with a beating heart, softly went up to her and undid her laces. He ripped off a hook and, without noticing it, tore her dress. Out of all the ribbons, the minute openings, and the tiniest folds of her clothing came tumbling onto the couch *his* prescriptions, *his* visiting cards and *his* photographs . . .

The doctor threw water on her face . . . She opened her eyes, raised herself on one elbow and, looking at him, grew thoughtful. Where am I? she wondered.

"I love you!" she moaned, having recognized him.

And her eyes, full of love and entreaty, came to rest on his face. She was gazing at him like a young, wounded animal.

"Whatever can I do?" he asked, having no idea at all what to do . . . He spoke in a voice that Marusya did not recognize, not in his monotonous staccato— but gently, almost tenderly . . .

Her elbow bent and her head fell back on the couch, but her eyes continued to gaze at him all the while. . . .

He remained standing before her, reading the entreaty in her eyes and feeling himself to be in a most frightful position. His heart was pounding, and something unprecedented and strange was taking place within his mind. A thousand unbidden memories came to life in his heated brain. Where did they spring from? Was it possible that they had been called forth by those eyes, with their love and entreaty?

He remembered his early childhood and the cleaning of his master's samovars. After the samovars and the cuffs, there came recollection of his patrons, and his patronesses in their heavy robes, and the parochial school where they had sent him to study because of his fine voice. The parochial school, with its birchings and the sand in the gruel, gave place to the seminary. At the seminary, Latin, hunger, dreams, reading, his love for the daughter of the Reverend-steward. He remembered how, against his patrons' wishes, he had run away from the seminary to the university. Without a penny in his pocket and in worn-out boots—what fascination lay in that escape! At the university he was glad to accept hunger and cold for the sake of his work . . . What a hard road!

In the end he had won, with his own brains he had opened a tunnel into life and passed through that tunnel, and . . . now what? He knows his trade superbly, reads a great deal, works a great deal and is ready to work day and night . . .

Toporkov looked out of the corner of his eye at the ten- and five-ruble notes which lay scattered on his desk; he thought of the 'ladies' from whom he had just received this money and blushed . . . Was it possible that just for these five-ruble notes and these 'ladies' he had trod this hard, laborious road? Yes, just for them . . .

And under the pressure of these memories his majestic figure shrank, his haughty bearing vanished, and his smooth face wrinkled.

"Whatever can I do?" he whispered again, looking into Marusya's eyes.

Those eyes put him to shame.

What if she had asked, "What have you accomplished and what have you gained during the whole time of your practice?"

Five-ruble and ten-ruble notes, and nothing else; study, life, peace, everything had been sacrificed to them. And they had given him in return princely quarters, a carefully chosen table, horses—everything, in a word, which goes by the name of comfort.

Toporkov remembered his seminary 'ideals' and his university dreams . . . and these easy chairs and this couch, upholstered in expensive velvet, these rugs completely covering the floor, these wall-sconces, this three-hundred-ruble clock appeared to him like a dreadful, impassable bog.

He stepped forward and lifted Marusya, bodily,

high up out of the bog in which she had been lying.

"Don't lie here!" he said, and turned his face away from the couch.

And as though in gratitude, a whole cascade of her wonderful flaxen hair poured down over his breast . . . Unfamiliar eyes sparkled close to his gold-rimmed spectacles. And what eyes! How he longed to touch them with his fingers!

"Let me have some tea!" she whispered.

.   .   .

Next day Toporkov was sitting with her in a first-class compartment. He was taking her to the south of France. What a strange man! He knew there was no hope of her recovery, knew it very well, like the five fingers of his own hand, yet he was taking her . . . The whole way he was tapping, listening, asking questions. He could not bear to believe his own findings and with all his strength he was endeavoring to tap out from her breast even the smallest ray of hope.

The money which up till yesterday he had been piling up so zealously was now strewn in huge doses along the way.

He would have given everything not to hear the cursed rattle in even one of the girl's lungs. Both he and she wanted so much to live! The sun had risen for them, and they were looking forward to the day . . .

But the sun did not save them from the darkness and . . . flowers will not bloom late in autumn!

Princess Marusya died, having lived less than three days in the south of France.

Toporkov has taken up his life as before since returning from France. As before he treats 'ladies' and accumulates five-ruble notes. However, one can see a change in him. When speaking to a woman he looks aside, into space. For some reason it frightens him to look into a woman's face . . .

Yegorushka is alive and well. He gave Kaleriya up and is now living at Toporkov's. The doctor took him into his home and dotes upon him. Yegorushka's chin reminds him of Marusya's chin, and because of this he allows Yegorushka to squander his five-ruble notes.

Yegorushka is perfectly contented.

The Little Trick

[1886]

It is a bright winter noontime. There is a hard, crackling frost, and as Nadyenka clings to my arm the curls on her temples and the down on her upper lip are covered with silver rime. We are standing on a high hill. A smooth rolling slope in which the sun is reflected as in a mirror stretches from our feet right down to the plain. There are little toboggans near us, covered with bright-colored cloth.

"Let's go down, Nadyenka Petrovna!" I beg her. "Just once! I assure you we'll end up safe and sound."

But Nadyenka is afraid. All that space from her little galoshes to the end of the icy mountain seems terrible to her, an immeasurably deep abyss. Her heart sinks and her breath comes in snatches when she looks down, when I merely suggest that she should sit in the toboggan. But supposing she were to risk flying down into the abyss! She would die, she would go out of her mind.

"Please come!" I say. "No need to be afraid! You know, this is timidity, cowardice!"

The Little Trick

In the end Nadyenka gives in, and I see by her face that she is giving in at the peril of her life. I set her down, pale and trembling, on the toboggan, put one arm around her and hurl myself with her into the gulf.

The toboggan flies like a bullet. The cutting air hits us in the face; it roars, it whistles in our ears, tears at us, bites us painfully out of malice, it wants to tear our heads from our shoulders. We can hardly breathe from the force of the wind. It seems as if the devil himself has caught us in his claws and is dragging us howling down to hell. The surrounding objects flow together into one long, swiftly rushing streak . . . Only a moment more and—it seems—we shall perish!

"I love you, Nadya!" I say in a low voice.

The toboggan begins to run more and more slowly, by now the howl of the wind and the hiss of the snow beneath us are not so terrible, our breath is no longer stopped, and at last we are down. Nadyenka is more dead than alive. She is pale, she is scarcely breathing . . . I help her to her feet.

"I wouldn't go down again for anything," she says, staring at me with large terror-filled eyes. "Not for anything in the world! I nearly died!"

In a little while she comes to herself and begins to look questioningly into my eyes. Was it really I who had spoken those four words, or had she only seemed to hear them in the uproar of the wind? And I stand beside her, smoking and attentively studying my glove.

She takes my arm and we stroll about the hill a long while. Evidently the riddle is giving her no peace. Were those words said or not? Yes or no? Yes or no? It is a question of pride, honor, life and happiness, a very important question, the most important in the world. Nadyenka is looking into my face impatiently, dejectedly, with a penetrating gaze—she answers me irrelevantly—she is waiting to see if I will speak. Oh, what a play of expression on that darling face, what a play! I can see she is struggling with herself. She has to say something, ask me something, but she cannot find the words, she is uncomfortable, frightened, and stirred by joy.

"Do you know what?" she says, not looking at me.

"What?" I ask.

"Let's . . . take one more ride."

We climb the ladder to the hill. Again I set a pale, trembling Nadyenka down on the toboggan, again we fly into the terrible abyss, again the wind roars and the snow hisses, and again at the fiercest and noisiest moment of the toboggan's flight I say in a low voice: "I love you, Nadyenka!"

When the toboggan stops, Nadyenka glances back up the mountain down which we have just slid, then she scrutinizes my face for a long time, listens attentively to my casual and quite unimpassioned voice, and everything about her, everything, even her muff and her hood, and her whole little figure—expresses the utmost bewilderment. And on her face is written: What happened? Who did say *those* words? Did he, or did I only seem to hear them?

The mystery worries her and tries her patience. The poor girl returns no answer to my questions; she is frowning and ready to cry.

"Don't you think we should go home?" I ask.

"Well, I . . . I like tobogganing," she says, blushing. "Can't we take one more ride?"

She "likes" tobogganing, yet at the same time, when she takes her place on the toboggan she is, just as the other times, pale, panting with fear and trembling.

We go down a third time, and I see her looking into my face, watching my lips. But I cover my mouth with my kerchief, cough, and when we are halfway down the hill, I have just time to say:

"I love you, Nadya!"

So the riddle remains a riddle! Nadyenka is silent, she is thinking about something . . . I accompany her home from the toboggan run; she slows her pace, and all the time she is waiting to see whether I will say those words to her. And I can see she is suffering, she is struggling with herself not to bring out: "The

wind couldn't have said them, it's impossible! And I
don't want the wind to have said it."

Next morning I receive a little note: "If you are
going to the toboggan run today, please call for me.
N." And from that day I begin going to the slide with
Nadyenka every day, and as we fly down on the toboggan, I utter the same words in a low voice every time.

"I love you, Nadya!"

Soon Nadyenka becomes addicted to this phrase,
as though to wine or morphine. She cannot live without it. It is as terrifying as ever, flying down the hill,
but now terror and danger lend a special fascination
to the words of love, words which as before make up
a riddle and torment her heart . . . The same two
are always suspect: the wind and I . . . Of the two
of us, who is declaring his love? She does not know,
but by now, apparently, it makes no difference to her;
if only she can get drunk, it makes no difference which
cup she drinks from.

One noontime I set out for the toboggan run alone;
after mingling with the crowd, I see Nadyenka approaching the hill, looking for me. Then she timidly
mounts the little ladder . . . How dreadful to ride
alone, oh, how dreadful. She is as white as snow, she
trembles, she walks as though to her execution,
but she walks without looking back, resolutely. Evidently she has decided in the end to put it to the test:
would she hear those marvelous sweet words when I

was not there? I see her, pale, her mouth open in terror, take her seat on the toboggan, close her eyes, and
having said farewell to the earth for ever, start off . . .
Whether Nadyenka hears those words, I do not know.
I only see her get up from the toboggan, exhausted and
weak. One can see from her face she herself does not
know whether she has heard anything or not. As she
was flying downhill she was too frightened to tell one
sound from another or to understand anything.

But then comes the spring month of March . . .
The sun shines more tenderly. Our icy hill grows dark,
loses its brilliance and in the end thaws out. We do.
no more tobogganing. There is no longer anywhere
for poor Nadyenka to hear those words, nor anyone
to say them, there is no wind to be heard, and I in-
tend to go off to Petersburg—for a long time, perhaps
for ever.

A day or two before my departure, I happen to be
sitting in the twilight in the little garden which is
separated from the courtyard of Nadyenka's house
by a high fence with nails . . . It is still rather cold,
there is still snow to be seen under the manure, the
trees are dead, but already it smells of spring, and the
rooks caw noisily as they settle down for the night. I
go up to the fence and look through a chink for a long
time. I see Nadyenka come out onto her porch and
cast a sorrowful, longing gaze on the sky . . . The
spring wind is blowing directly into her pale, sad

face . . . It reminds her of the wind that roared at us on the mountain, when she heard those four words, and her face grows very, very sad, a tear rolls down her cheek . . . And the poor girl stretches out both hands, as if begging this wind to bring those words to her once more. And, after waiting for the wind to blow, I say with it in a low voice:

"I love you, Nadya!"

Good lord, what is happening to Nadyenka! She cries out, smiles all over her face and stretches out her hands against the wind—radiant, happy and so beautiful.

And I go away to pack . . .

That was a long time ago. Nadyenka is married by now. She was married off—or she chose him herself, it makes no difference—to the secretary of the Trusteeship Department of the Nobility*, and she already has three children.

She did not forget that we went tobogganing together long ago, and that the wind carried to her the words "I love you, Nadyenka." It is now the happiest, most touching and beautiful memory of her life.

But now, when I am older, I no longer understand why I said those words, nor why I played the trick . . .

---

* Dvoryanskaya opeka—a prerevolutionary institution set up to watch over the interests of the nobility, both as individuals and as a class.

Verochka

[1887]

Ivan Alexeyevich Ognev remembered how the glass door jangled that particular August evening when he had opened it and walked out into the terrace . . . At the time he was wearing a light caped overcoat and a wide-brimmed straw hat, the same one which now lay in the dust under his bed along with his high leather boots. In one hand he held a large package of books and notebooks, and in the other, a thick knotty staff. Behind the door, lighting the way for him with a lamp, stood the owner of the house, Kuznetsov, a bald-headed old man with a long gray beard, wearing a piqué jacket as white as snow. The old man was smiling warmly and nodding his head.

"Goodbye, old fellow!" Ognev called to him.

Kuznetsov put the lamp on a little table and went out onto the terrace. Two long thin shadows passed over the steps toward the flowerbeds, wavered, and their heads came to rest on the trunks of the lime trees.

"Goodbye and thank you again, my dear!" said Ivan

Alexeyich. "Thank you for your hospitality, and your affection and your love . . . I shall never, never forget your hospitality! You are wonderful, and your daughter is wonderful, and every one of your people here is kind and cheerful and generous. I can't begin to tell you what magnificent people you are!"

From an excess of emotion and under the influence of the brandy he had just been drinking, Ognev spoke in a singsong, seminarian's voice, and was so carried away that he expressed his feelings by blinking his eyes and shrugging his shoulders even more than by his words. Kuznetsov, also a little drunk and very moved, reached out toward the young man and kissed him.

"I'm so at home here, just like one of your hounds!" Ognev went on. "I've been hanging around your place nearly every day, I've passed the night here a dozen times, and it's dreadful to remember now how much of your brandy I've drunk. But more than anything else, Gavril Petrovich, I thank you for your assistance and help. Without you I should probably have been poring over these statistics until October. So I shall write in my preface: 'I consider it my duty to express my gratitude to Mr. Kuznetsov, Chairman of the Zemstvo of N—— district, for his very kind assistance.' There is a brilliant future for statistics! Give my deepest respects to Vera Gavrilovna, and tell the doctors, and the two inspectors and your secretary that I shall never forget their help! And now, old man, let's put our arms round one another and take a last kiss."

Ognev, almost in tears, kissed the old man again and started down the stairs. On the lowest step he looked back and asked:

"Shall we ever see each other again some day?"

"God knows!" the old man answered. "Never, probably!"

"Yes, that's right! There is nothing to tempt you to Petersburg, and for my part, I shall hardly be making another trip into this district. Well, goodbye!"

"You should leave your books here!" Kuznetsov called after him. "What fun do you get out of carrying such a weight? I could send them to you tomorrow by one of my men."

But Ognev was no longer listening and was rapidly leaving the house behind him. His heart, warmed by the liquor, was happy and warm and melancholy all at the same time . . . He walked along, and he thought how often it happens in life that one meets wonderful people and what a pity it was that nothing remains of these meetings but memories. Sometimes a flight of cranes will pass like a flash across the horizon and a light wind carries back their wailing, rapturous cry, but a minute later, no matter how greedily you may peer into the blue distance, you will not see a sign of them nor hear a sound—in just the same way people, with their faces and words, will flash into our life and melt into our past, leaving nothing behind but insignificant traces in the memory. After living ever since the spring in N—— district, and visiting the hospitable Kuznetsovs nearly every day, Ivan Alexeyevich had grown as used to the old man and to his daughter and to the servants as though they were his own family; he knew, down to the minutest details, the whole house, the comfortable terrace, the windings of the paths, the silhouettes of the trees above the kitchen and the bathhouse; but in another minute he would be past the wicket gate and it would all turn into a memory and lose its real meaning for him forever, and a year or two would pass and all these dear images would grow dim in his mind just like the inventions and creations of fantasy.

There is nothing in life dearer than people! thought Ognev, with emotion, as he strode down the alley towards the garden gate. Nothing!

It was quiet and warm in the garden. It smelled of mignonette, tobacco flowers and heliotrope, which had not yet finished blooming in the flowerbeds. The spaces between the bushes and the trunks of the trees were filled with mist—light, delicate, saturated with moonlight—and what stayed long in Ognev's memory were the wisps of fog, like ghosts, that floated, softly but clearly visible, one after the other, across the paths.

Verochka

The moon was high above the garden, but below it, patches of transparent fog drifted somewhere to the east. The whole world seemed to be made up only of black silhouettes and wandering white shadows, and Ognev, looking at the mist in the moonlit August evening, thought almost for the first time in his life that he was looking not at reality, but at a painted backdrop where clumsy pyrotechnists, trying to light up the garden with white Bengal flares, sat behind the bushes filling the air with white smoke along with the light.

When Ognev came to the garden gate, a dark shadow detached itself from the low picket fence and came to meet him.

"Vera Gavrilovna!" he exclaimed happily. "Are you here? And I have been hunting and hunting for you, I wanted to say goodbye . . . Goodbye, I am leaving!"

"So early? But it's only eleven o'clock."

"No, it's time! Five versts* to go, and I still have to pack. I have to get up early tomorrow . . ."

In front of Ognev stood Kuznetsov's daughter Vera, a girl of twenty-one, looking sorrowful as usual, carelessly dressed and attractive. Girls who daydream a great deal and spend the whole day lying about indolently reading everything that comes into their hands, who are subject to boredom and melancholy, are generally careless about their clothes. This lazy negligence in dress adds a charm of its own to those

* A verst is approximately two-thirds of a mile.

[89]

whom nature has endowed with taste and an instinct for beauty. At any rate, whenever he thought about the pretty Verochka afterwards Ognev was never able to imagine her otherwise than in an oversize blouse, creased into deep folds at the waist but still not touching her figure, with a stray lock falling over her forehead from her high-piled hair, and with that red knitted shawl with its fringe of shaggy balls which every evening, like a flag in still weather, hung dispiritedly from Verochka's shoulders, and in the daytime lay crumpled up either in the vestibule beside the men's caps or on a chest in the dining room, where the old cat unceremoniously slept on it. This shawl and the creases in her blouse had their own aura of easy idleness, domesticity and good nature. Perhaps because Ognev was so fond of Vera, he could read something warm, easy and simple in each little button and flounce, something beautiful and poetic, that is lacking in so many women who are without a sense of beauty, insincere and cold.

Verochka was finely proportioned, she had a classic profile and beautiful wavy hair. She seemed a real beauty to Ognev who had seen very few women in his life.

"I am leaving!" he said, bidding farewell to her at the garden gate. "Don't think unkindly of me! Thank you for everything!"

In that same singsong seminarian's voice as he had used to the old man, blinking his eyes and shrugging his shoulders in the same way, he began to thank Vera for her hospitality, her warm friendship and her kindness.

"I wrote to my mother about you in every letter," he said. "If only everyone were like you and your dear father, there would be no more everyday humdrum life here below, but a never-ending carnival. All you people are splendid! Everyone is so simple and warm and sincere."

"Where are you going now?" asked Vera.

"I'm going to see my mother in Orel now; I shall stay with her about two weeks and then I'll be off to Petersburg, to work."

"And afterward?"

"Afterward? I shall be working all winter, and in the spring I shall be on the way to some other place in this district to collect material. Well, may you be happy, and live a hundred years . . . don't think unkindly of me. We shall never see each other again."

Ognev bent down and kissed Verochka's hand. Then in silent agitation he straightened out his cape, arranged his package of books more comfortably and after a short silence said, "The mist is really thick!"

"Yes. You haven't forgotten any of your things?"

"What? No, I don't think so . . ."

For a few seconds Ognev remained there in silence, then he turned awkwardly to the wicket gate and walked out of the garden.

"Wait a minute, I will see you as far as our wood," said Vera, following him.

They went down the road. Here the trees no longer hid everything from sight and it was possible to see the sky and the far distance. Nature was hiding herself behind a dim transparent haze, as though covered by a veil through which her beauty peered gaily out; patches of mist, a little denser and whiter than the rest, lay unevenly over the stooks of corn and the bushes or floated in wisps across the road, pressed close to the ground as if trying not to hide the distant view. Through the haze one could see the whole road as far as the wood, with the dark ditches on either side and the little bushes growing in them which kept the wisps of fog from straying. At half a verst from the garden gate loomed the dark shape of the Kuznetsovs' woodland.

Why did she come along with me? Now I shall be obliged to see her back home! thought Ognev. But after glancing at Vera's profile he smiled tenderly and said, "I don't feel like going away in such lovely weather! This evening is really so romantic, with moonlight, stillness and all the trimmings. Do you know something, Vera Gavrilovna? I've lived twenty-nine years in this world, but there has never been a single

romance in my life. In my whole life there has never
been one single romantic event, so that I know about
rendezvous, and avenues of sighs, and kisses only
by hearsay. It isn't normal! You don't notice this gap in
your life when you are sitting in your furnished
room in the city, but here, in the open air, you feel it
very strongly . . . Somehow it's—insulting!"

"Why should you be like this?"

"I don't know. Probably because all my life I never
had time, or perhaps I just never happened to meet the
kind of women who . . . On the whole I have very
few friends, and I never go visiting."

For about three hundred paces the young people
kept silent. From time to time Ognev glanced at Verochka's bare head and at her shawl, and one after another the spring and summer days came to life again
in his mind. That was when, far away from his gray
Petersburg room and rejoicing in the affection of these
fine people, in nature and in his satisfying work,
he had been too busy to notice how the morning
sunrises gave place to the evening sunsets, and how one
after another first the nightingale, then the quail and
a little later the corncrake ceased to sing, foretelling
the end of summer . . . The time had flown unnoticed, which meant that he was living a wonderful, easy life . . . He began to recall aloud how reluctantly he had made the journey here to N—— district at the end of April, rather hard up, quite unac-

customed to traffic and people, and expecting to meet
here boredom, loneliness, and indifference to Statistics
which, in his opinion, now held first place among the
sciences. He had arrived in town on an April morning
and had stopped at the inn of an Old Believer,* Rya-
bukhin, where for twenty kopecks a day he was given
a clean and airy room on condition that he would
smoke only out of doors. When he had rested and made
inquiries as to who held the post of Chairman of the
District Council, he had immediately set out on foot
to the house of Gavril Petrovich. He had to walk five
versts through lush meadows and groves of young trees.
The skylarks quivered under the clouds, filling the air
with silver sound, and rooks skimmed over the green
plowed fields, sedately and decorously fluttering their
wings.

Good Lord, Ognev mused then, can the air always be like this here, or does it just smell like this
today in honor of my arrival?

Anticipating a chilly reception of his business call
he had entered Kuznetsov's house rather timidly, looking about him through narrowed eyes and shyly tugging at his beard. The old man at first knitted
his brows and could not understand what this young
man with his statistics wanted from the district council, but when it had been explained to him at great

* A sect that followed the old Russian Orthodox creed and
maintained a strict and old-fashioned way of life.

length what this statistical material was and where it was to be collected, Gavril Petrovich cheered up, began to smile and with childish curiosity began looking through his copybooks. That very evening Ivan Alexeyich was already sitting down to supper in Kuznetsov's house and rapidly growing tipsy on strong brandy. As he looked at the placid faces and lazy movements of his new friends, he felt in his whole body that sweet, drowsy languor which inclines one to sleep and stretch and smile. And his new friends were examining him good-naturedly, asking him if his father and mother were living, and how much he earned a month, and did he often go to the theatre? . . .

Ognev recalled his travels about the various districts, his picnics and fishing trips, an excursion with the whole company to a convent of novices to see the Mother Superior, Marfa, who gave each of the guests a beautiful little embroidered purse; he recalled heated, interminable, purely Russian arguments, when the debaters, spluttering and banging their fists on the table, misunderstood and interrupted each other and, without even noticing it, contradicted themselves in every sentence, continually changed the subject, and, after arguing for two or three hours, laughed at themselves:

"What the devil are we arguing about! We began on one thing, ended up with another!"

"And do you remember how you and I and the doctor went on horseback to Shestovo?" Ivan Alexeyevich said to Vera as he walked beside her toward the forest. "That time we met a 'holy fool?' I gave him a five-kopeck piece, but he crossed himself three times and threw my five kopecks into the rye. Oh Lord, I'm taking so many impressions away with me, that if it were possible to roll them all up into one solid lump they would make a wonderful gold nugget! I just don't understand why intelligent and sensitive people crowd together in the capitals and don't come out here? Is there really more space and truth on the Nevsky Prospect and in the big damp houses than there is here? Really, my furnished rooms, filled with artists and scientists and journalists from top to bottom, always seemed like a ridiculous prejudice to me."

A small narrow footbridge with little posts at the corners crossed the path within twenty paces of the wood; it always served the Kuznetsovs and their guests as a little terminus to their evening strolls. From here those who wished to could invoke the forest echo, and the road could be seen disappearing into the dark cutting in the forest.

"Well, here's the bridge," said Ognev. "This is where you turn back . . ."

Vera stopped and drew in her breath.

"Let's sit down a little while," she said, seating herself on one of the corner posts. "People usually do sit together awhile, when they are saying good-bye."

Ognev took a place near her on his bundle of books and went on talking. She was breathing heavily after the walk and did not look directly at Ivan Alexeyich but rather to one side, so that he could not see her face.

"Just suppose, after ten years, we suddenly meet each other again," he said. "What shall we be like then? You will be the respected mother of a family and I shall be the author of some kind of respected, thick and utterly useless collection of statistics, like forty thousand other collections. We shall meet and reminisce about the old days . . . We are conscious of reality now, we are filled with it and stirred by it, but when we meet then we shall no longer remember the date, nor the month, nor even the year when we saw each other at this little bridge for the last time. Very likely, you will be quite different . . . Listen, you will be different, won't you?"

Vera started and turned her face toward him.

"What?" she asked.

"I was just asking you . . ."

"I'm sorry, I didn't hear what you were saying."

Only then did Ognev notice the change in Vera. She was pale, she struggled for breath, and the shuddering of her breathing communicated itself to her hands and her lips and her head, and from her coiffure not one lock of hair, as always, but two had escaped onto her forehead. . . . She was obviously avoiding his eyes and, in trying to hide her agitation, she was now loosening the little collar of her dress, as though it were cutting her neck, and pulling her red shawl from one shoulder to the other . . .

"You seem to be cold," said Ognev. "It's not really good for you to be sitting about in this mist. Why don't you let me take you back to the house?"

Vera said nothing.

"What is the matter?" Ivan Alexeyich said, smiling. "You don't say a word, you don't answer my questions. Are you not well, or are you angry? Eh?"

Vera had been pressing her palm hard against the cheek which was turned toward Ognev, and all at once she snatched it sharply away.

"What a horrible situation to be in . . ." she whispered with an expression of great pain in her face. "Horrible!"

"What is so horrible?" asked Ognev, shrugging his shoulders and not hiding his astonishment. "What is the matter?"

Still breathing heavily, her shoulders shaking, Vera turned her back on him, looked up at the sky for half a minute, and said, "I must tell you something, Ivan Alexeyich . . ."

"I'm listening."

"Perhaps it will seem queer to you . . . you will be astonished, but it makes no difference to me . . ."

Ognev once again shrugged his shoulders and prepared to listen.

"You see, this . . ." began Verochka, bending her head and plucking with her fingers at the fringe of her shawl . . . "You see, this is what I . . . wanted to tell you . . . It will seem very odd and foolish, but I . . . I can no longer . . ."

Vera's words turned into a vague mumbling and suddenly she began to cry. The girl covered her face with her shawl, bent still lower and wept bitterly. Ivan Alexeyich grunted in embarrassment and, dumbfounded, not knowing what to say or do, looked hopelessly about him. His own eyes, unaccustomed to weeping and tears, began to smart.

"Well, what next!" he began murmuring in perplexity. "Vera Gavrilovna, what is all this about, that's what I want to know? My dear, are you . . . are you ill? Or has someone offended you? Do tell me, maybe I . . . could help . . ."

When he ventured cautiously to draw her hands away from her face, trying to comfort her, she smiled up at him through her tears and burst out, "I . . . I love you!"

These simple and ordinary words were spoken in a simple human tongue, but Ognev turned away from

Vera in great confusion; he got to his feet and immediately felt his confusion turn to fear.

The melancholy, the cordiality, the sentimental
mood occasioned by his leave-taking and the brandy,
vanished abruptly, and were replaced by a harsh, unpleasant feeling of embarrassment. As though his heart
had suddenly turned inside out he looked askance at
Vera; in declaring her love for him, she had thrown
away completely the remoteness which is so becoming
to a woman, and she now seemed to him less tall,
plainer and darker.

What is all this? he thought, terrified. And yet . . .
do I love her, or don't I? That is the question!

But she, now that the most important and difficult
thing had at last been said, breathed lightly and
freely. She, too, stood up and, looking straight into
Ivan Alexeyich's face, began to talk quickly, irrepress-
ibly and ardently.

Just as a man who is suddenly overwhelmed by terror cannot afterwards remember the exact order of
sounds accompanying the catastrophe which stuns him,
even so Ognev could not remember Vera's words and
phrases. His memory retained only the substance of
her speech, herself, and the sensation her speech produced in him. He remembered her voice, as though it
were choked and slightly hoarse from excitement, and
the extraordinary music and passion of her intonation.
Crying, laughing, the tears glittering on her eyelashes,

she was telling him that even from the first days of their acquaintance she had been struck by his original- ity, his intellect, his kind intelligent eyes, with the aims and objects of his life; that she had fallen pas- sionately, madly and deeply in love with him; that whenever she had happened to come into the house from the garden that summer and had seen his coat in the vestibule or heard his voice in the distance, her heart had felt a cold thrill of delight, a foretaste of happiness; even his silliest jokes made her laugh helplessly, and in each figure of his copybook she could see something extraordinarily clever and grandiose; his knotted walking stick seemed to her more beautiful than the trees.

The forest and the wisps of fog and the black ditches alongside the road seemed to fall silent, listening to her, but something bad and strange was taking place in Ognev's heart . . . Vera was enchantingly beautiful as she told him of her love, she spoke with eloquence and passion, but much as he wanted to, he could feel no joy, no fundamental happiness, but only compas- sion for Vera, and pain and regret that a good human being should be suffering because of him. The lord only knows whether it was his bookish mind that now began to speak, or whether he was affected by that irresistible habit of objectivity which so often prevents people from living, but Vera's raptures and suffering seemed to him only cloying and trivial. At the same time he was outraged with himself and something whispered to him that what he was now seeing and hearing was, from the point of view of human nature and his personal happiness, more important than any statistics, books or philosophical truths . . . And he was annoyed and blamed himself even though he himself did not understand why he was to blame.

To complete his discomfort, he really did not know what to say to her, but he had to say something. He did not have the strength to say frankly "I do not love you," nor could he say "Yes," because no matter how hard he searched, he could not find even the smallest spark of love in his heart.

He was silent, but she meanwhile was saying that there could be no greater happiness for her than to see him, follow him, even this very moment, wherever he wished, to be his wife and helpmate; that she would die of grief if he left her . . .

"I can't stay here!" she said, wringing her hands. "I'm sick of the house and this forest and the whole atmosphere. I can't stand this everlastingly quiet, aimless life. I can't stand our dull, insipid people who are all exactly alike, like so many drops of water! They are all warm and good-natured because their stomachs are full and they don't suffer, they don't struggle . . . But I long for just those big gray houses where they do suffer and are desperate from toil and poverty . . ."

It all seemed cloying and trivial. When Vera had finished, he still did not know what to say, but it was impossible to remain silent and he began to mumble.

"Vera Gavrilovna, I am very grateful to you, although I feel that I do not deserve any such . . . feelings . . . on your part . . . Secondly, as an honest man, I must tell you that happiness can only be based on a true balance . . . such as when both sides . . . are equally in love . . ."

But all at once Ognev was ashamed of his mutterings and fell silent. He felt his face must look stupid, guilty and dull, that it was strained and tense . . . Vera had probably managed to read the truth in his face, for she suddenly became very grave, turned pale and hung her head.

"You must forgive me," muttered Ognev, unable to endure the silence. "I have such a high regard for you, that . . . it's painful!"

Vera turned abruptly away and began to walk quickly back toward the estate. Ognev followed her.

"No, there is no need for you to come!" said Vera, waving him away. "Don't come, I can get home by myself . . ."

"No, but just the same . . . It wouldn't be right not to see you off . . ."

Everything Ognev had said, down to his last word, seemed to him detestable and trite. The feeling of guilt grew upon him with every step. He was angry, and clenched his fists and cursed his own coldness and his inability to behave properly to women. Trying to arouse himself, he looked at Verochka's lovely figure, at her braided hair and at the prints which her little feet left in the dusty path, he recalled her words and her tears, but it all merely touched him, it did not move him to the heart.

Oh, it really is impossible to make oneself fall in love! he tried to persuade himself, and at the same time he thought, Whenever shall I fall in love if I don't force myself? I'm almost thirty already! I've never met a better woman than Vera and I never shall . . . Oh, this beastly old age! Old age at thirty!

Vera walked ahead of him ever faster and faster, not looking back and keeping her head lowered. It seemed to him that she had shrunk with grief, her shoulders looked narrower . . .

Imagine what is going on in her heart now! he thought, looking at her back. Most likely she is so hurt and ashamed she wants to die! Oh Lord, there is enough life, poetry and true sense in all of this to touch a heart of stone, but I . . . I'm a fool and an idiot!

At the wicket gate Vera glanced quickly at him and then, stooping and wrapping herself in her shawl, went swiftly away down the path.

Ivan Alexeyich was left alone. As he walked back toward the wood, he went slowly; now and again he paused and glanced back at the wicket gate, his whole attitude conveying the impression of one who cannot believe himself. His eyes searched along the path for

Vera's footprints, and he could not believe that the girl whom he had been so fond of had just told him she loved him and that he had so crudely and coarsely "refused" her! For the first time in his life he had learned by experience how little a man depends on his own free will, and had understood, from his own case, the position of a decent and sincere man who against his own will is the cause of cruel and undeserved suffering to his fellow men.

His conscience hurt him, and, when Vera had disappeared, it began to seem as though he had lost something very dear and intimate which he would never find again. He felt that a part of his youth had slipped away from him with Vera and that the moments he had so vainly wasted would never again be repeated.

As he came up to the little bridge, he stopped and was lost in thought for a while. He wanted to find the cause of his strange coldness. It was clear to him that it lay within himself, and not outside. He frankly admitted to himself that this was not that rational coldness which intelligent people so often boast of, not the coldness of an egoistical fool, but simply a feebleness of the spirit, an inability to appreciate beauty profoundly, an early old age, which had come upon him through his upbringing, through the disorderly struggle to make a living, and his solitary life in furnished rooms.

From the little footbridge he walked on slowly, as if against his will, into the forest. There, where the rays of moonlight made shining patches here and there in the thick black darkness, where he was aware of nothing except his own thoughts, he felt a passionate desire to have back what he had lost.

And Ivan Alexeyich remembered, too, how he had gone back again. Urging himself on by memories, forcibly conjuring Vera up in his imagination, he had walked rapidly back to the garden. It was no longer misty along the road or in the garden, and a brilliant moon looked down from the sky as though washed clean; only the east was misty and lowering. Ognev remembered his cautious steps, the dark windows, the heavy scent of heliotrope and mignonette. His old friend Karo, amicably wagging his tail, came up to him and sniffed his hand . . . It was the only living creature to see him as he walked two or three times around the house, stood for a while under Vera's dark window and, giving it up for lost, with a deep sigh walked out of the garden.

An hour later he was in the little town; exhausted, jaded, resting his body and burning face against the gate of the inn, he pounded on the iron bolt. Somewhere in the town a dog barked, half-awakened, and as though in reply to his knocking someone began beating on the cast-iron alarm-plate* by the church.

* In every village there was a bell or a sheet of iron hanging

"Gadding about all night . . ." grumbled the Old Believer innkeeper as he opened the gate in his long nightgown, like a woman's. "You'd better be saying your prayers instead of gadding about."

Ivan Alexeyich went into his room, sank down on the bed and looked at the fire for a long, long time; then he shook his head and began to pack . . .

near the church, to be rung or beaten on in case of fire or other alarm. Presumably this was a warning of the fire Ivan Alexeyich is looking at in the last paragraph.

The Beauties

[1888]

I remember, when I was a schoolboy in the fifth or sixth class of the gymnasium, I went on a journey with my grandfather from the village of Bolshaya Krepkaya, in the province of Don, to Rostov-on-Don. It was a day in August, burning hot, oppressively monotonous. My eyelids were stuck together, my mouth was parched from the heat and the dry scorching wind which drove clouds of dust toward us. I did not want to look at anything, or to talk, or to think, and when our dozing driver, the Ukrainian Karpo, flicked my cap with his whip as he urged on his horse, I made no protest, did not utter a sound—only, coming out of my daze, gazed meekly and despondently into the distance. Wasn't there a village to be seen through the dust? We stopped to feed the horses in a large Armenian village called Bakchi-Salakh, at the home of a wealthy Armenian, an acquaintance of my grandfather's. Never in my life had I seen anyone more grotesque than this Armenian. Imagine a little cropped head with thick, low-arching eyebrows, a hawklike nose, long gray whiskers, and a wide mouth from which a long cherry-wood *chibouk* protruded. This little head was clumsily stuck onto a scraggy hump-backed torso clothed in a fantastic costume: a dock-tailed red jacket and wide bright-blue Turkish trousers called *sharivari*. The figure kept its feet wide apart as it walked, shuffled its slippers, talked without taking the *chibouk* out of its mouth and conducted itself with real Armenian dignity—never smiling, its eyes goggling, and endeavoring to pay as little attention to its guests as possible.

There was neither wind nor dust inside the Armenian's house, and yet it was just as unpleasant, stifling and monotonous as on the steppe and along the road. I remember sitting in the corner on a green chest, covered with dust and overcome by the heat. The bare wooden walls and furniture and the floors painted with ocher smelled of dry wood scorched by the sun. Wherever you looked there were flies, flies, flies everywhere. . . . My grandfather and the Armenian were talking in low voices about grazing land and manure and sheep. . . . I knew that it would take a whole hour to prepare the samovar, and that my grandfather would be at least an hour drinking his tea, and afterwards would lie down and sleep for two or three hours, that a quarter of my day would be passed in waiting, and after that there would again

be the heat, the dust, the jolting roads. I listened to
the murmuring of the two voices, and it began to seem
to me that I had been looking for a long, long time at
the Armenian, the china-cupboard, the flies, and the
windows through which the sun came blazing in . . .
that I would go on looking at them until far into the distant future . . . and I was seized with hatred for the
steppe, for the sun, for the flies . . .

A Ukrainian woman wearing a shawl brought in a
tray with tea-things and the samovar. The Armenian
strolled out into the passageway and shouted:

"Mashya! Hurry up and serve the tea! Where are
you? Mashya!"

Quick footsteps were heard, and a girl of about sixteen entered the room, wearing a simple calico dress
and a white kerchief on her head. She stood with
her back to me while she washed the china and poured
out the tea, and I noticed only that she was slim-
waisted, barefoot, and that her long trousers almost
covered her small bare heels.

Our host invited me to have tea. As I sat down at the
table, I glanced at the girl's face as she handed me
my glass, and all at once I felt as though a breeze had
blown through my soul, carrying away with it all the
impressions of the day, the dust, the tedium. I saw
the enchanting features of one of the most beautiful
faces I had ever encountered in real life or seen in my
dreams. A real beauty stood before me, and I recog-

nized this from the first glance as I would recognize a flash of lightning.

I am ready to swear that Masha or, as her father called her, Mashya, was a perfect beauty, but I have no way of proving it. Sometimes it happens that clouds pile up in confusion on the horizon, and the sun, hiding behind them, will paint them and the whole sky in all the colors of the rainbow: crimson, orange, gold, violet and a dull rose. One little cloud looks like a monk, another like a fish, a third like a Turk in his turban. A glow covers a third of the sky; it glitters on the church cross and on the glass panes of the manor house; it is reflected in the river and the puddles; it quivers on the trees; far far away against the background of the sunset a flock of wild duck is flying off to pass the night somewhere . . . And the young herdsman who is driving his cattle along, and the surveyor riding in his gig across the dam, and the gentlemen out for a stroll—they are all looking at the sunset and one and all they find it extraordinarily beautiful, but no one knows and no one can explain wherein the beauty lies.

It was not I alone who found the Armenian girl beautiful. My grandfather, an old man of eighty, a harsh man generally indifferent to women and the beauty of nature, looked tenderly at Masha for a full minute, and asked, "Is this your daughter, Avet Nazarych?"

"My daughter. This is my daughter," answered his host.

"A fine girl!" my grandfather praised her.

A painter would have called the young Armenian girl's beauty classical and severe. It was exactly the kind of beauty whose contemplation, heaven knows why, makes you feel certain you are looking at perfect features, that the hair, eyes, nose, mouth, neck, breast, and all the movements of the young body are fused together into one well-ordered, harmonious accord, in which nature has not made the slightest error. Somehow it seems to you that to be perfectly beautiful, a woman must have just such a nose as Masha's, straight and slightly aquiline, just such large dark eyes, just such long lashes, just such a dreamy gaze; that her dark ringlets and eyebrows are as suited to the tender pallor of her brow and cheeks as green rushes to a quiet stream. Masha's white neck and young breast are but slightly developed, yet it seems to you, a supreme creative talent would be needed to sculpt them. You go on looking at her, and little by little you are overcome by a longing to tell Masha something unusually pleasing, candid, lovely—just as lovely as she is herself.

At first I was hurt and ashamed that Masha did not pay the slightest attention to me and kept her gaze lowered all the time; a kind of special air, happy and proud, seemed to set her apart and hid her jealously from my eyes.

It is because I'm all dusty and sunburned, I thought, and because I am still a boy.

But afterward I gradually forgot about myself and was entirely overcome by the awareness of her beauty. I even forgot about the boredom of the steppe and the dust; I did not hear the buzzing of the flies, I did not notice the taste of the tea, and I was conscious of nothing except that a beautiful girl was standing across the table from me.

Her beauty affected me in a rather strange way. Masha did not arouse desire in me, nor enjoyment nor delight, but a deep yet at the same time sweet sadness. This sadness was vague and dim like a dream. For some reason I was sorry for myself, for my grandfather, for her father, and for the Armenian girl herself, and I had a feeling as though all four of us had wasted something important and vital for our lives which we should never find again. My grandfather was melancholy too. He no longer talked about manuring and sheep, but was silent and gazed thoughtfully at Masha.

After tea my grandfather lay down for a nap, and I went out of the house and sat on the little porch. The house, like all the houses in Bakchi-Salakh, stood in full sun; there was no tree, no veranda, no shade at all. The Armenian's big courtyard, overgrown with goosefoot and dwarf mallow, was full of life and gaiety de-

spite the intense heat. Beyond one of the law wattle
fences which crossed the big yard here and there, they
were threshing grain. Around a post driven into the
exact center of the threshing floor trotted a dozen
horses, harnessed together in a single row to form the
long radius of a circle. Their Ukrainian driver, in a
long waistcoat and wide *sharivari*, walked alongside
them, cracking his whip and crying out in the tone of
one who wishes to tease his horses and boast of his
power over them, "A-a-a-ahhh, you devils! A-a-a-ahhh, a
plague on you! Are you scared of something?"

The horses, bay, white and piebald, who had no idea
why they were being made to run round and round in
the same place and trample the straw, trotted reluctantly as though it were beyond their strength, and
waved their tails indignantly in the air. The wind
lifted whole clouds of golden chaff from beneath their
hoofs and carried it far away across the fence.
Women with rakes swarmed around the high, freshly
built stacks and bullock-carts moved forward, while
beyond the stacks, in another courtyard, a dozen more
of the same kind of horses trotted around their post
and the same kind of Ukrainian driver cracked his
whip and made fun of his horses.

The steps on which I was sitting were scorching
hot; here and there, from the heat, a wood glue was
oozing out of the flimsy railings and the window
frames. Little red insects were crowded together in

the stripes of shade under the steps and beneath the shutters. The sun blazed down on me, on my head, on my chest and on my back, but I hardly noticed it, and was conscious only that behind me in the entrance hall and the inner rooms bare feet were pattering over the plank floors. When she had put away the tea-things, Masha ran down the steps, making a gust of wind past me, and flew like a bird toward a little sooty out-building, probably the kitchen, from which came a smell of roast mutton and the sound of angry Armenian voices. She vanished into the dark doorway, and in her place an old hunched-over Armenian woman, red-faced and wearing green *sharivari*, appeared on the thresh-old, angrily scolding someone. Soon Masha came out all flushed from the heat of the kitchen, with a big loaf of black bread on her shoulder; bending gracefully under the weight of the bread, she darted across the yard towards the threshing-floor, slipped over the fence and vanished behind the bullock-carts, swallowed up in a cloud of golden chaff. The Ukrainian, who had been urging his horses on, lowered his whip, fell quiet, and for a moment looked in silence towards the carts. Then, when the young Armenian girl again appeared for a moment beside the horses and vaulted over the fence, his eyes followed her, and he cried out to his horses as though in real distress:

"A-a-a-ah, the devil take you!"

And all the time I was constantly listening for the

sound of her bare feet, and watching her skimming over the yard with her grave preoccupied face. She would run past me down the steps, fanning me with a breeze, first to the kitchen, then to the threshing floor, and then through the gate, and I hardly had time to turn my head to look after her.

And the oftener she flashed before my eyes in her beauty, the deeper became my melancholy. I was sorry for myself, and for her, and for the driver following her sadly with his eyes every time she slipped through the cloud of chaff towards the bullock-carts. Only God knows whether on my part it was envy of her beauty; or whether I regretted that this girl was not mine and never would be, and that I was a stranger to her; or whether I vaguely felt that her uncommon beauty was a mere accident, serving no purpose, and, like everything on earth, short-lived; or whether my sadness was perhaps the singular feeling aroused in men by the contemplation of perfect beauty.

The three hours of waiting passed unnoticed. It seemed to me I had hardly had time to look at Masha when Karpo went down to the stream, let the horse splash in the water, and was already putting on the harness. The wet horse snorted with glee and banged its hoofs against the shafts. Karpo yelled at it: "Gi-i-i-dap, there!" My grandfather awoke. Masha opened the squeaking gate for us; we took our seats in the cart and made our way out of the yard. We moved along without saying a word, as though angry with one another.

When after two or three hours Rostov and Nakhichevan' appeared in the distance, Karpo, who had been silent all the way, suddenly looked round and said:

"What a wonderful girl the Armenian has!"

And he laid his lash across the horse.

Another time, when I was already a university student, I was going south by train. It was May. At one of the stations—it was between Belgorod and Kharkov, I believe—I got out of the carriage to take a short walk up and down the platform.

The evening dusk already lay on the station garden, on the platform and on the countryside. The station building concealed the sunset, but it was evident from the topmost puffs of smoke, which came from the engine colored with a soft rosy light, that the sun had still not altogether set.

I noticed as I strolled along the platform that most of the passengers who had got out were either walking or standing near a single second-class carriage, and there was a certain expression on all their faces as if some noted person or other were sitting in this carriage. Among the curious whom I met around the carriage there also happened to be my train companion, an artillery officer, a clever fellow, warm and likable, like all those we meet casually and briefly on a journey.

"What are you looking at?" I asked.

He did not answer, but directed me with his eyes to the figure of a woman. She was still a young girl, about seventeen or eighteen, wearing Russian dress, with her head uncovered and a cloak thrown carelessly over one shoulder; she was not a passenger, but probably the daughter or sister of the stationmaster. She stood beside the carriage window chatting with an elderly woman passenger. Before I had time to take in what I saw, I was suddenly overcome by the feeling I had experienced once before in the Armenian village.

The girl was an extraordinary beauty, and neither I nor any of those who were also watching her had any doubt about it.

If I were to describe her appearance feature by feature, in the accepted way, then indeed her only beauty was her fair, thick, wavy hair, flowing loose and bound only with a little black ribbon. All the rest was either irregular or quite ordinary. Her eyes squinted a little, either from a particular way of flirting or from nearsightedness; she had an irresolute snub nose, a small mouth, a weak and indistinctly outlined profile; her shoulders were narrow for her age, but nonetheless this girl created the effect of a perfect beauty, and, as I looked at her, I was convinced that the Russian face does not require a strict regularity of feature to seem beautiful. Moreover, if this girl had been given another nose, a regular and plastically faultless one like the Armenian girl's in place of her own turned-up one, it seems her face would have lost all its charm.

As she stood at the window and chatted, hugging herself occasionally against the evening damp, the girl would now and again glance round at us, now stand with her hands on her hips, now put her hands up to her head to smooth her hair; she talked, she laughed, her face revealing now astonishment, now terror, so that I cannot recall a moment when her body and her face were perfectly still. The whole secret and the magic of her beauty lay precisely in those slight, infinitely graceful movements: in her smile, in the play of her face, in her swift glances at us, in the accord between the delicate grace of these movements and her youth, her freshness, her pure soul, reflected in the sound of her laugh and her voice, and that tender weakness we love so much in children, in birds, in fawns and in young trees.

Hers was the beauty of a butterfly, made for waltzing and fluttering across the garden, for laughter and gaiety—having nothing in common with serious thought, grief or quiet. And, it seemed, it needed only a stiff breeze to skim over the platform, or a shower of rain, and the fragile body would immediately wilt, and her capricious beauty float away like the pollen of a flower.

"So-o-o-o . . ." muttered the officer with a sigh as we walked back to our carriage after the second bell.

What the meaning of this "So-o-o-o" was I would not venture to judge.

Perhaps he was sad and did not feel like leaving this lovely girl and the spring evening for a stuffy railway carriage; or it may be that he, like myself, was unaccountably sorry for her, and for himself, and for me, and for all the other passengers who were returning, listlessly and unwillingly, to their carriages. As we passed by the station-office window at which sat a pale red-haired telegraph operator with high curls and a mottled, high-cheekboned face, the officer sighed and said:

"I bet that telegraphist is in love with that pretty little thing. To live in the wilds under the same roof with that ethereal creature and not fall in love with her would be beyond a man's power! But what misery, my friend, what mockery, to be a round-shouldered, disheveled, dull, respectable, sensible man and fall in love with this pretty light-headed girl who pays no attention to you whatever! Or even worse: suppose the telegraphist *has* fallen in love with her, but happens to be married, and that his wife is just such a round-shouldered, disheveled, respectable person as himself . . . what torture!"

A conductor was standing near our carriage, leaning his elbows on the railing of the rear platform and looking toward the side where the beauty stood, and his flabby, unpleasantly bloated face, ravaged by drink, tired out by sleepless nights in the tossing carriages, wore an expression of tender emotion and profound sadness, as if he saw in the girl his own youth, happiness, temperance, purity, his wife and his children—as if he regretted from the depths of his heart that this girl was not his and that, with his premature old age, his clumsiness and his fat greasy face, he was as far removed from the ordinary happiness of humanity, of his passengers, as from heaven itself.

The third bell rang, the whistles blew, and the train started off lazily. First the conductor, then the stationmaster flashed by our windows, and then the garden, and the beauty with her artful-child's wonderful smile . . .

When I put my head outside and looked back I could see her, after she had watched the train leave, walk down the platform past the window where the telegraphist was sitting, smooth her hair, and then go running into the garden. The station no longer concealed the west, the country was in full view; but the sun had already set, and feathers of black smoke streaked the green velvet of the winter wheat. It was mournful in the evening air, and in the darkening sky, and in the railway carriage.

Our conductor came into the compartment and began putting on the lights.

Big Volodya and Little Volodya

[1893]

"I want to drive myself, do let me! I'll sit next to the coachman!" said Sofia L'vovna loudly. "Wait a minute, coachman, I'll sit on the box with you."

She was standing up in the sleigh, while her husband Vladimir Nikitich and her childhood friend Vladimir Mikhailich held her by the arms so she would not fall. The troika rushed on swiftly.

"I told you you shouldn't have given her cognac," whispered Vladimir Nikitich with annoyance to his companion. "Really, what am I going to do with you!"

The colonel knew from experience that with women like his wife Sofia L'vovna, a mood of boisterous, rather drunken gaiety would usually be followed by hysterical laughter and then weeping. He was afraid that now when they got home he would have to busy himself with compresses and medicine drops instead of going to bed.

"Whoa!" cried Sofia L'vovna. "I want to drive!"

She was genuinely gay and exultant. For the past

two months, since the very day of her wedding, she had been tormented by the thought that she had married Colonel Yagich for convenience and, as the saying goes, *par dépit*; today, however, in the out-of-town restaurant, she had at last realized that she loved him passionately. In spite of his fifty-four years he was so well-built, so agile, so lissom, he made puns and joined in the gypsy girls' songs so nicely. Really, nowadays the older men were a thousand times more interesting than the young ones and old age and youth seemed to have exchanged roles. The colonel was older than her father by two years, but could this fact have any meaning if, in all conscience, his vitality, high spirits and freshness were immeasurably greater than her own, though she was only twenty-three years old?

Oh, my darling! she thought. You are wonderful!

In the restaurant she had realized as well that not even a spark of her former feeling remained any longer in her heart. She now felt completely indifferent to her childhood friend Vladimir Mikhailich, or Volodya to give him his familiar name, whom only yesterday she had loved to the point of madness and despair. All evening he had seemed to her spiritless, sleepy, uninteresting, insignificant, and the unconcern with which he customarily avoided paying the restaurant bills this time disgusted her, and she could hardly restrain herself from saying to him: "If you have no money, you should stay at home." The colonel alone paid.

Perhaps because trees, telegraph poles and snow drifts were flashing by before her eyes, all kinds of different thoughts were running through her head. She was thinking: the restaurant bill came to a hundred and twenty, and the gypsies—a hundred, and tomorrow, if she liked, she might scatter a thousand rubles to the winds, yet two months ago, before her marriage, she had not had a penny of her own, and had had to turn to her father for the slightest trifle. What a complete change in her life!

Her thoughts were very confused, and she remembered too how, when she was about ten years old, Colonel Yagich, who was now her husband, had courted her aunt and everyone at home had said he had ruined her; and how indeed her aunt often came down to dinner with tear-stained eyes and would leave home every now and then; and it was said of her that the poor thing could find no peace anywhere. He was very handsome then and had had unusual success with women, so that everyone in town knew him and stories were told about him, how he rode around every day paying visits to his lady admirers as a doctor visits the sick. And even now, in spite of his gray hair, wrinkles and spectacles, his lean face, particularly in profile, sometimes looked magnificent.

Sofia L'vovna's father was an army doctor and had

served at some time in the past in the same regiment
as Yagich. Volodya's father was also an army doctor,
and he too had served in the past in the same regiment
as her father and Yagich. Despite his amorous adven-
tures, often very complicated and stormy, Volodya
was a splendid student; he had finished his university
course with high honors and had now chosen to spe-
cialize in foreign literature and was said to be writing
a dissertation. He now lived in barracks, with his
father, the army doctor, without any money of his own
although he was already thirty years old. When they
were children, Sofia L'vovna and he lived in different
quarters but under the same roof, and he often went
to her home to play and together they were taught to
dance and to speak French; but when he grew up and
turned into a finely built, very handsome youth, she
felt shy with him at first and then fell madly in love
with him and loved him till the last, until she married Yagich. Volodya too had had unusual success with
women, almost since his fourteenth year, when women
who deceived their husbands with him made the excuse to themselves that Volodya was a little boy. Not
long ago someone used to tell the story that, when he
was a student, living in furnished rooms near the university, whenever anyone knocked on his door, his
footsteps would be heard approaching the door and
then would come the apology in a low tone, *"Pardon,
je ne suis pas seul."* Yagich used to go into raptures

over him and gave him his blessing for a great future, as Derzhavin* did to Pushkin, and apparently loved him. They would both play billiards or piquet in silence by the hour together and if Yagich went anywhere in a troika he took Volodya with him, while Volodya initiated only Yagich into the mysteries of his dissertation. Earlier, when the colonel was younger, they had often found themselves in the position of rivals but were never jealous of each other. In society, where they went about together, Yagich was called Big Volodya, and his friend Little Volodya.

There was one more person in the sleigh besides Big Volodya, Little Volodya and Sofia L'vovna—Margarita Alexandrovna, or Rita as she was called, a cousin of Yagich's wife, a girl already past thirty, very pale, with black eyebrows, and pince-nez, who was smoking one cigarette after another even in the biting frost; there were always ashes on her breast, on her knees. She talked with a nasal twang, drawling every word; she was a cold woman, who could drink liquor and cognac to her heart's content without getting drunk, and who liked to tell doubtful jokes, in a limp and tasteless manner. At home she read heavy magazines from

* Gavril Romanovich Derzhavin (1743–1816), most celebrated Russian poet of the eighteenth century. In 1815, a year before his death, the old man judged a poetry competition in the Petersburg lyceum, in which the young Pushkin, then sixteen, had submitted an ode in imitation of Derzhavin. He embraced the boy, praised him to the skies and foretold a great future for him.

morning till night, strewing ashes all over them, or chewing on frosted apples.

"Sonya, stop making such a fuss," she said in a singsong voice. "Really, it's too stupid."

The troika slowed down as they approached the city gate; houses and people flashed by and Sofia L'vovna pressed close to her husband, grew quiet, and became absorbed in her thoughts. Little Volodya was sitting opposite. Now her light, happy reflections were mixed with gloomy ones. She thought: this man who was sitting opposite had known that she loved him, and certainly believed the gossip that she had married the colonel *par dépit*. She had never once told him she loved him and she did not want him to know of it and had hidden her feelings; but it was plain from the look on his face that he understood her perfectly, and her pride suffered. But more humiliating than anything else in her position was the fact that after her marriage this Little Volodya had suddenly begun to pay attention to her, which had never happened before, and would sit with her for hours in silence or chatting about trifles and now, when they rode out in the sleigh, without saying a word to her he would lightly press her foot with his or squeeze her hand; obviously he had only wanted her to get married; and it was plain that he despised her and that she aroused only a certain kind of interest in him, as a wicked and dishonorable woman. And as her feelings of triumph and love for her husband became mixed with humiliation and hurt pride, she felt suddenly wildly mischievous, and then she wanted to sit on the box and cry out and whistle . . .

Just as they were passing close by a convent, they heard the peal of a great twenty-ton bell. Rita crossed herself.

"Our Olya is in that convent," said Sofia L'vovna, and she too made the sign of the cross and shivered.

"Why did she go into a convent?" the colonel asked.

"*Par dépit,*" Rita answered crossly, obviously hinting at Sofia L'vovna's marriage to Yagich. "It's quite the rage now, this *par dépit.* It's a challenge to the whole world. She was a giggling tease and a wild flirt, she cared for nothing but balls and beaux, and all at once—look what happens! She has surprised everyone!"

"That's not true," said little Volodya, turning down his fur collar and showing his handsome face. "There was no *par dépit* here, but sheer terror, if you want to put it that way. Her brother Dmitri was banished to hard labor, and now no one knows where he is. And her mother died of grief."

He raised his collar again.

"Olya did right," he added tonelessly. "To have to live like a foundling, especially with such a jewel as Sofia L'vovna—just think of it!"

Sofia L'vovna heard the contemptuous tone of his voice and wanted to say something offensive to him, but she held her tongue. The same wildly mischievous feeling again seized her; she sprang to her feet and cried out in a tearful voice, "I want to go to Matins! Coachman, turn back! I want to see Olya!"

They turned back. The peal of the convent bell was very deep, and something in it seemed to remind Sofia L'vovna of Olya and her life. The bells in other churches began to ring too. When the coachman stopped the troika, Sofia L'vovna jumped down from the sleigh and alone, with no one accompanying her, went quickly toward the gate.

"Be quick, please!" her husband shouted. "It's already late!"

She passed through the dark gate, then down the alley which led from the gate to the main church, and the light snow crunched under her feet and the bell rang out above her head and seemed to penetrate her whole being. Here was the church door; then three steps down, a vestibule, with pictures of the saints on both sides, where it smelt of juniper and incense; then again a door and a woman's dark figure opening it and bowing very low to her . . . In the church the service had not yet begun. One nun was moving along before the sanctuary screen, lighting the candles on their stands, another was lighting the chandelier. Here and there near the columns and the side aisles, black figures were standing motionless.

That means they will stand just the way they are now, without moving, till morning, thought Sofia

L'vovna, and it seemed to her dark and cold and oppressive here—more oppressive than a graveyard. She
glanced round with a feeling of depression at the motionless frozen figures, and suddenly her heart was
wrung. Somehow she had recognized Olya in one of
the nuns, small in stature, with thin shoulders and a
black cowl on her head, although Olya when she entered the convent had been plump and had seemed
taller. Hesitant and very nervous for some reason, Sofia
L'vovna approached the novice, glanced over her shoulder at her face and recognized Olya.

"Olya!" she said, and struck her hands together,
hardly able to speak in her agitation. "Olya!"

The nun recognized her at once and raised her eyebrows in amazement, and her pale, freshly washed
pure face and even the little white kerchief which was
visible under her cowl seemed to shine with happiness.

"What a miracle from heaven," she said and she too
struck her thin, pale little hands together.

Sofia L'vovna hugged her tight and kissed her,
afraid at the same time she might smell of liquor.

"We were just driving past and we remembered
you," she said, breathlessly as though from a fast walk.
"Good heavens, how pale you are! I—I'm so glad to
see you. Well, how are you? What is it like? Do you
miss us?"

Sofia L'vovna looked round at the other nuns and
then went on in a low voice, "There have been lots of

changes at home . . . I married Yagich, Vladimir Nikitich, you know. I'm sure you remember him . . . I'm very happy with him."

"Well, thank God. And is your father well?"

"Yes, he is. He often thinks about you. Olya, do come to us for the holidays. Are you listening?"

"I will," said Olya and smiled slightly. "I will come on the second day."

Sofia L'vovna without knowing why began to cry and for a moment wept silently, then she dried her eyes and said, "Rita will be very sorry she didn't see you. She's with us too. And Volodya is here. They are just by the gate. How happy they would be if you would come out and see them! Let's go out and see them; the service hasn't started yet."

"Let us go," Olya agreed.

She crossed herself three times and went with Sofia L'vovna toward the door that led out.

"So you are happy, you say, Sonyechka* ?" she asked as they passed beyond the gate.

"Very."

"Well, thank God."

Big Volodya and Little Volodya got down from the sleigh when they caught sight of the nun and greeted her respectfully; they were both obviously touched by her pale face and black nun's habit, and they were both pleased she remembered them and had come out

* Sonya, Sonyechka . . . familiar forms of Sofia.

to greet them. Sofia L'vovna wrapped her in a rug so she should not be cold and threw a fold of her own fur coat around her. The tears she had just shed had eased and lightened her heart and she was happy that this noisy, restless and essentially dissolute night had unexpectedly ended so cleanly and mildly.

To keep Olya near her longer, she suggested, "Let's take her for a drive! Sit down, Olya, we'll only go a little way."

The men expected the nun to refuse—the devout do not usually ride in troikas—but to their amazement she agreed and sat down in the sleigh. And when the troika darted away to the city gate, they were all silent and tried only to make her warm and comfortable, and each was thinking how she had been before and how she was now. Now her face was impassive, almost expressionless, cold, pale and transparent as though water and not blood were flowing in her veins. Yet two or three years ago she had been plump and rosy and had talked about fiancés and laughed uproariously at the merest trifle . . .

Near the city gate the troika turned back. When it drew to a halt beside the convent ten minutes later, Olya got down from the sleigh. The church bells were now chiming in the bell tower.

"God bless you," said Olya and bowed down to the ground in the convent fashion.

"Do come and see us, Olya."

"I will, I will."

She walked quickly away and soon disappeared within the dark gate. And for some reason, when the troika started off afterward they all felt very, very sad. No one spoke. Sofia L'vovna felt a weakness in all her limbs, and her heart sank; it seemed to her stupid, tactless and almost blasphemous that she had forced the nun to sit in the sleigh and take a drive in drunken company. The wish to deceive herself left her along with her intoxication, and it was already plain to her that she did not love her husband and never could, that it was all nonsense and stupidity. She had married for convenience, because he was, in the expression of her schoolgirl friends, madly rich, and because it would be awful to stay an old maid, like Rita, and because she was fed up with her doctor-father, and wanted to spite Little Volodya. If she could only have guessed when she was getting married that it would be so hard to bear, so terrible and so ugly, she would not have agreed to marry for all the riches in the world. But what was done could not be undone now. She would have to put up with it.

They went home. As she lay down in her warm soft bed and drew the covers over her, Sofia L'vovna remembered the dark nave of the church, the smell of incense and the figures by the columns, and it was terrible to think that these figures would remain standing there motionless all the time she was asleep. Matins would last a long, long time, then there would come the hours of vigil, afterward the Mass and the regular church service . . .

But there really is a God, most likely He does exist, and I will certainly have to die; that means that sooner or later one must think of one's soul and eternal life, like Olya. Olya is saved now, she has decided all the questions for herself . . . But what if there is no God? Then her life will have been wasted. Or will it be wasted? Why is it wasted?

But in another minute another thought crept into her head:

There is a God, death will certainly come, one must think of one's soul. If Olya were suddenly to see her own death this very minute, she wouldn't be terrified. She is ready. But the main thing is, she has already decided the questions of life for herself. There is a God . . . yes . . . But can't there possibly be another way out besides entering a convent? Really, going into a convent . . . means renouncing life, destroying it . . .

Sofia L'vovna became a little frightened; she hid her head under the pillow.

"I mustn't think about this," she whispered. "I mustn't . . ."

Yagich was walking up and down on the rug in the adjoining room, softly jingling his spurs and thinking of something or other. The thought suddenly occurred to Sofia L'vovna that this man was close and dear to her for one thing only—his name was Vladimir too. She sat up in bed and called tenderly, "Volodya!"

"What's the matter?" her husband called back.

"Nothing."

She lay down again. She could hear bells, probably from the very same convent; they reminded her again of the church nave and the dark figures. Thoughts of God and of inevitable death whirled about in her mind, and she wrapped the covers over her head that she might not hear the pealing. She reflected that before old age and death overtook her a long, long lifetime would still have to be dragged out, and day after day she would have to put up with the nearness of the man she did not love, who had by now come into the bedroom and was going to bed. And she would be obliged to stifle within her her hopeless love for another—a young, fascinating, and it seemed to her, quite extraordinary man. She glanced at her husband and wanted to say goodnight to him, but instead she suddenly burst into tears. She was annoyed with herself.

"Well, the *music* is beginning!" Yagich said, pronouncing it mu*sique*.

She did quiet down, but not until much later, about ten o'clock in the morning. She stopped crying and shaking all over; instead her head began to ache violently. Yagich was hurrying to get ready for late mass and in the next room he was grumbling at his orderly who was helping him to dress. He came into the bedroom once, softly jingling his spurs, and took something, and later on a second time, already in his epaulettes and decorations, limping ever so slightly from rheumatism, and it seemed to Sofia L'vovna, for some reason, that he walked and looked around like a beast of prey.

She heard Yagich ringing up on the telephone.

"Please be good enough to connect me with the Vasilyevski barracks!" he said, and in a moment, "Vasilyevski barracks? Please ask Dr. Salimovich to come to the phone . . ." and in another moment: . . . "Whom am I speaking to? You, Volodya? Very glad to hear you. My dear, ask your father to come over to our house at once, my wife is in very bad shape after our outing yesterday . . . He's not in, you say? Hmm . . . Thank you. Wonderful . . . I'm very much obliged . . . *Merci.*"

Yagich came into her bedroom a third time, bent down to his wife, made the sign of the cross over her, gave her his hand to kiss—the women who had loved him had always kissed his hand and he was accustomed to it—and said that he would be back for dinner. And he left.

At twelve o'clock the maid announced that Vladimir Mikhailovich had arrived. Sofia L'vovna, staggering from weariness and headache, quickly put on her striking new fur-trimmed lilac robe and hastily pinned up her hair somehow; she felt an inexpressible tenderness in her heart and was trembling with joy and terror lest he should go away. If only she could set eyes on him!

Little Volodya had come visiting, in the most correct manner, in a frock coat and white cravat. When Sofia L'vovna came into the drawing room he kissed her hand and expressed his sincere regret that she was not feeling well. Afterward, when they had sat down, he complimented her on her robe.

"It upset me, seeing Olya yesterday," she said. "At first I felt horrible, but now I envy her. She is an indestructible rock, no one will ever be able to move her from her place; but was there really no other way out for her, Volodya? Do you really have to bury yourself alive to solve the riddle of life? That is death, you know, not life."

A tender expression appeared on Volodya's face at the mention of Olya.

"You're an intelligent person, Volodya," said Sofia L'vovna. "Teach me how to do exactly what she did. Of course I'm not a believer, and I couldn't join a convent, but there must be something that will mean as much. My life is not easy," she went on after a moment's silence. "Tell me . . . Say something convincing. Just one word will do."

"One word? Here you are: Tararaboomdeay."

"Volodya, why do you despise me?" she asked him spiritedly. "You use such particularly—forgive me—

silly, dandified language when you talk to me, not the kind people use with their friends or with respectable women. You're a great success as a scholar, you love science, why don't you ever talk to me about science? Why? Am I unworthy of it?"

Little Volodya was annoyed; he made a wry face and said, "What do you want to talk about science for all of a sudden? Perhaps you'd like to discuss the constitution? Or sturgeon with horse-radish, maybe?"

"Well, all right, I'm a worthless, wretched, unprincipled, dim-witted woman . . . I've made hundreds and hundreds of mistakes, I'm psychopathic and depraved and I deserve to be despised for it. But look, Volodya, you are ten years older than I and my husband is thirty years older. I grew up under your very eyes, and if you had wanted to you could have made anything you liked out of me, even an angel. But you"—her voice shook—"you treat me dreadfully. Yagich married me when he was already old and you . . ."

"Now that's enough, that's enough," said Volodya, sitting closer to her and kissing both her hands. "Let's leave the Schopenhauers to philosophize and prove everything just as they like, but as for ourselves, let's kiss these little hands."

"You do despise me, and if you only knew how I suffer from it!" she said uncertainly, knowing beforehand that he would not believe her. "If you only knew how I want to be different, and begin a new life! I think of it with rapture," and she did indeed shed a few rapturous tears as she spoke. "To be a good, honest, pure human being—not to lie—to have a goal in life!"

"Now, now, now, please don't put on an act! I don't like it!" said Volodya, and his face took on a capricious expression. "Good lord, you might as well be on the stage. Let's behave like real people."

So that he would not grow angry and leave, she began making excuses for herself and to please him forced herself to smile. Again she began talking about Olya and how she, too, wished to solve the problem of her life and become a real human being.

"Tara . . . ra . . . *boom*deay," he sang under his breath. "Tara . . . ra . . . *boom*deay!"

And suddenly he grasped her round the waist. She herself put her hands on his shoulders, not really knowing what to do, and for a minute looked with ecstasy as though in a daze, into his clever, mocking face, at his forehead, his eyes, his magnificent beard . . .

"You've known for a long time that I love you," she confessed; she blushed agonizingly and felt that even her lips were contorted with shame. "I do love you. Why do you torture me?"

She closed her eyes and kissed him hard on the lips, and for a long time, perhaps a full minute, she could not bring herself to end the kiss, even though she knew it was quite improper, that he might be con-

[144]

demning her himself, that a servant might come in . . .

"Oh, how you torture me!" she repeated.

Half an hour later, having achieved what he wanted, he was sitting in an armchair having a snack while she knelt in front of him looking greedily into his face, and he was telling her she looked like a pet dog waiting to be thrown a scrap of ham. Afterward he sat her on his knee and, rocking her like a baby, sang:

"Tara . . . raboomdeay. Tara . . . raboomdeay!"

When he was getting ready to leave, she asked him in a passionate voice, "When? Today? Where?"

And she held out both her hands to his mouth, as though longing to draw forth his answer even with her hands.

"Today would hardly be convenient," he said, after thinking it over for a moment. "But tomorrow perhaps."

They separated. Before dinner Sofia L'vovna drove to the convent to see Olya, but there they told her that Olya was away somewhere reading the psalter for a woman who had died. She went from the convent to her father but did not find him at home either; afterward she changed carriages and drove for a while up and down the streets and byways, quite aimlessly, and drove about in that way till evening. And for some reason she was reminded of her own aunt with the tear-stained eyes, who could find no peace anywhere.

And that night they again drove out in a troika and listened to the gypsies in the out-of-town restaurant. And when they passed by the convent again, Sofia L'vovna remembered Olya and was terrified by the thought that for girls and women of her class there was no other way out but endlessly driving about in troikas and lying, or entering a convent and mortifying the flesh . . . And the next day there was another rendezvous, and again Sofia L'vovna drove about the town alone in a carriage and was reminded of her aunt.

In a week Little Volodya broke off with her. And after that life went on as before, just as uninteresting, sad and sometimes even agonizing. The colonel and Little Volodya played for hours at billiards and piquet, Rita told jokes in her limp and tasteless manner, and Sofia L'vovna rode about constantly in a carriage and begged her husband to take her out in a troika.

Calling at the convent almost every day, she wearied Olya complaining to her of her unbearable suffering, she wept and felt at the same time that something unclean, pitiful and shabby entered the cell with her. Mechanically, in the tone of one reciting a prepared lesson, Olya would tell her that none of this mattered in the slightest, that it would all pass and God would forgive her.

A Visit to Friends

[1898]

A letter came one morning:

MY DEAR MISHA,

You have utterly forgotten us; do come and pay us a visit
right away. We are longing to see you. We both beseech
you on our knees, come today, let us see your bright eyes.
We are waiting impatiently.

TA and VA.

KUZMINKY, June 7

The letter was from Tatyana Alexeyevna Losev who
ten or twelve years ago, when Podgorin was living at
Kuzminky, used to be called Ta, for short. But who
was this Va? Long conversations came back to Podgorin—happy laughter, novels, strolls in the evening,
and a whole flower garden of girls and young women
who were living in and around Kuzminky then. And
he remembered a simple, lively, intelligent face with
freckles that went well with the dark red hair—this
was Varya, or Varvara Pavlovna, Tatyana's close
friend. She had finished her medical studies and was
working in a factory somewhere the other side of Tula,

[149]

and now, evidently, she had arrived in Kuzminky as a guest.

Darling Va! thought Podgorin, giving himself up to memories. What a wonderful girl!

Tatyana, Varya and he were almost the same age, but he had been a student then, while they were already grown-up girls, old enough to be married, and they looked upon him as a little boy. And although he was a lawyer now and beginning to go gray, they still called him Misha, thought of him as a very young man and said that he had had no experience of life yet.

He was very fond of them, but seemed fonder of them in retrospect than in reality. The present state of affairs was unfamiliar to him, difficult to understand and strange. And this short, playful letter was strange too, a letter they had probably spent a long time composing, with effort, and Tatyana's husband, Sergei Sergeyich, had probably been standing right behind her as she wrote . . . Kuzminky had come to her as a dowry only six years ago, but it had already been ruined by this same Sergei Sergeyich. And now whenever the time came to settle accounts with the bank or to make a payment on the mortgages, they turned to Podgorin, as a lawyer, for advice, and on top of that they had already asked him twice for loans. This time, too, they obviously wanted either advice or money from him.

He no longer felt drawn to Kuzminky as in former

days. It was cheerless there. There was no longer any laughter, or hubbub, or happy carefree faces, or secret meetings on quiet moonlit nights—but above all there was no longer youth; and it was all enchanting, probably, in memory only. . . . Besides Ta and Va, there was also Na, Tatyana's sister Nadezhda, whom they referred to, either in jest or in earnest, as his fiancée. She had grown up under his very eyes; they had expected him to marry her, and at one time he had been in love with her and intended proposing to her— but here she was, already twenty-five and still he had not married her . . .

Strange how it all came about, he was thinking now, as he reread the letter with discomfiture. But I can't possibly *not* go, they would be hurt.

The fact that he had not visited the Losevs for a long time lay heavy on his conscience. And after he had walked up and down his room thinking things over, he forced himself to a decision and resolved to go and stay with them for two or three days, fulfill his obligation and afterward feel free and at peace with himself, at least until next summer. He told his servants, as he was getting ready to leave for the Brest railway station after breakfast, that he would be back in three days.

It was a two-hour ride from Moscow to Kuzminky, and after that twenty minutes by horse from the station. From the station one could see Tatyana's woodlands and three tall narrow summer cottages which Losev had begun to build but never finished, having embarked on various questionable transactions in the first years after his marriage. These summer cottages had ruined him, along with sundry other business ventures and frequent trips to Moscow, where he could lunch at the *Slavyansky Bazaar*, dine at the Hermitage, and wind up his day on Malaya Bronnaya Street or at the Zhivodyorka night club with the gypsies (he called this "Giving oneself a lift"). Podgorin himself drank, sometimes heavily, and was promiscuous with women, but casually, coldly, without finding any pleasure in it, and he was disgusted when other men abandoned themselves passionately in front of him. He could not understand people who felt more free at Zhivodyorka than they did at home beside decent women, and he did not care for such people; it seemed to him that they wallowed in all sorts of uncleanness which clung to them like burrs. He did not like Losev either and considered him uninteresting, an absolute lazy good-for-nothing, and he had more than once felt nauseated in his company.

Just past the woods, he was met by Sergei Sergeyich and Nadezhda.

"My dear old fellow, why have you forgotten us like this?" Sergei Sergeyich said, kissing him three times and then clasping him round the waist with both arms. "You no longer care for us, dear friend!"

He had big features, a thick nose and a skimpy fair beard; he parted his hair on the side, like a merchant, in order to look like a simple, honest Russian. When he talked, he breathed right into his listener's face, and when he was silent, he breathed heavily through his nose. His well-fed body and excessive weight hampered him, and in order to breathe more easily he was continually sticking out his chest; this gave him a haughty appearance. Nadezhda, his sister-in-law, looked quite ethereal beside him. She was slender, very fair and pale, with kind, affectionate eyes; Podgorin really did not know whether she was beautiful or not, for he had known her from her childhood and had grown used to her appearance. She was in a white dress now, open at the throat, and the effect of her white, long, bare neck was new to him and not altogether pleasing.

"My sister and I have been waiting for you since morning," she said. "Varya is staying with us, and she has been waiting too."

She took his arm and suddenly burst out laughing without any reason and gave a low, happy cry, as though all of a sudden charmed by some thought or other. The fields, thick with winter rye standing without a ripple in the still air, and the forest, lit up by the sun, were beautiful; it was as though Nadezhda had noticed this only just now, as she walked beside Podgorin.

"I've come to spend three days with you," he said. "You must forgive me, I could not get away from Moscow earlier."

"It's wrong, it's wrong of you to forget all about us," said Sergei Sergeyich in good-humored reproach. " *'Jamais de ma vie!'* " he added suddenly and snapped his fingers.

He had a mannerism, startling for the person he was speaking to, of inserting in the form of an exclamation some phrase or other having nothing at all to do with the conversation, and snapping his fingers at the same time. And he was constantly imitating somebody; if he rolled his eyes, or carelessly tossed back his hair, or sank into pathos, this meant he had been to the theatre the day before, or at a dinner where there had been speech-making. Now he was walking like a man with gout, with little mincing steps and without bending his knees—probably he was imitating someone now, too.

"You know, Tanya didn't believe you would come," said Nadezhda. "But Varya and I had a premonition; somehow I knew you would come on this very train."

" *'Jamais de ma vie!'* " repeated Sergei Sergeyich.

The other ladies were waiting on the terrace in the garden. Ten years ago Podgorin—he was a poor student then—had coached Nadezhda in mathematics and history in return for his board and lodging, and

Varya, who was attending a girls' college, took Latin lessons from him on the side. But Tanya, already a beautiful grown-up girl by then, thought of nothing but love, desired only love and happiness, desired it passionately, and was waiting for the bridegroom she dreamed of day and night. And now, when she was over thirty, as beautiful and as striking as ever, in a full peignoir, with plump white arms, she thought only of her husband and her two little daughters; and her expression suggested that, even though she might be talking and smiling, nonetheless she was keeping her thoughts to herself, nonetheless she was on watch over this love and her right to this love, and was ready at any moment to hurl herself on any enemy who might wish to take her husband and children from her. She loved her husband ardently, and it seemed to her that the love was mutual; yet jealousy, and fear for her children, tortured her ceaselessly and prevented her from being happy.

After the noisy greetings on the terrace, everyone except Sergei Sergeyich went into Tatyana's room. The sun's rays could not penetrate here, through the lowered blinds; it was twilight, so that all the roses in a large bouquet seemed of one color. They made Podgorin sit down in an old armchair by the window. Nadezhda sat on a low footstool at his feet. He knew that besides the soft reproaches, jests, and laughter which reminded him so much of the past, there would still be an unpleasant discussion about promissory notes and mortgages—this was unavoidable—and he reflected that it might be better to talk over business matters right now rather than to put them off; get it over with quickly and—afterward—get away into the garden, into the open air . . .

"Shouldn't we talk about business first?" he said. "What is there new at Kuzminky? Is everything prospering in the state of Denmark?"

"Things are bad with us at Kuzminky," Tatyana answered and sighed mournfully. "Oh, our affairs are in such a dreadful state, it seems they couldn't be worse," she said, pacing up and down the room in agitation. "Our estate is up for sale, the auction is set for the seventh of August, it has already been advertised all over, and buyers are arriving here, going all through the rooms, looking at everything . . . Everybody has the right now to go into my room and look around. It may be right, according to the law, but it humiliates me; it's profoundly insulting. We have nothing to pay with and no one to borrow from any longer. In a word, it's horrible, horrible! I swear to you," she went on, halting in the middle of the room, her voice trembling and her eyes filling with tears, "I swear to you by all I hold sacred, by my children's happiness, I can't live without Kuzminky! I was born here, this is my nest, and if they take it away from me I shall not survive it. I shall die of grief."

"It seems to me you're taking too gloomy a view," said Podgorin. "Everything will turn out all right. Your husband will take a job with the government, you will settle into a new routine and start a new life."

"How can you say that!" cried Tatyana. Now she looked very beautiful and strong, and her face and her whole figure expressed most vividly her readiness to hurl herself at any moment on any enemy who might wish to take her husband, her children and her nest away from her. "What kind of new life would that be! Sergei is looking for a position, he has been promised a place as tax inspector somewhere in the district of Ufa or Perm, and I am ready to go anywhere, even to Siberia; I am prepared to live there ten, twenty years, but I must be sure that sooner or later, in spite of everything, I shall come back to Kuzminky. I can't live without Kuzminky. I can't and I don't want to. I don't want to!" she cried and stamped her foot.

"Misha, you're a lawyer," said Varya. "You're sharp, and it's up to you to advise us what to do."

There was only one truthful and rational answer, "There's nothing to be done." But Podgorin could not bring himself to say it outright, and he mumbled irresolutely, "This will have to be thought over . . . I'll think about it."

There were two men in him. It had fallen to him as

a lawyer to handle some rough cases, and in the law court and with his clients he conducted himself haughtily and always expressed his opinion plainly and sharply. Among his everyday companions he affected rudeness, but in his personal, intimate life, among those close to him or with people he had known a long time, he revealed an unusual delicacy, with them he was shy and sensitive and unable to speak bluntly. A single tear, a side glance, a lie or even a clumsy gesture was enough to make his heart contract and his will power evaporate. Now Nadezhda was sitting at his feet, and her bare neck displeased him, and this disturbed him; he even wanted to go home. One day a year ago he had run into Sergei Sergeyich at a certain lady's on Bronnaya Street, and now he felt awkward in front of Tatyana, as though he himself had been an accomplice in the betrayal. This conversation about Kuzminky presented him with a great problem. He was accustomed to having all delicate and unpleasant questions resolved by a judge or a jury or simply by some article of law; whenever a question was presented to him personally, for his own solution, he was at a loss.

"Misha, you're our friend, we all love you like one of the family," Tatyana went on, "and I will tell you quite frankly: you are our only hope. Will you for God's sake tell us what to do? Maybe we should submit an application somewhere? Maybe it's still not too

late to transfer the estate to Nadya's or Varya's name?
. . . What shall we do?"

"Help us, Misha, help us," said Varya, lighting a
cigarette. "You were always so bright. You've lived
very little, you still haven't had any experience of
life, but you have a good head on your shoulders . . .
You will help Tanya, I know."

"I'll have to think it over . . . Possibly I may
think up something."

They went out for a stroll in the garden and afterward in the fields. Sergei Sergeyich came along too.
He took Podgorin by the arm and continually pulled
him on ahead, apparently intending to talk something
over with him, probably the bad state of affairs. But
to walk beside Sergei Sergeyich and talk to him was
torture. Every now and again he kissed Podgorin—
always three times—took his arm, clasped him around
the waist, and breathed into his face; and it seemed
as if he were covered with a sugary glue and in a minute would be stuck fast to you; the expression in his
eyes, hinting that he needed something from Podgorin, that he was on the point of asking him for something, created a painful impression as though he were
taking aim with a pistol.

The sun had set, it began to grow dark. Here and
there along the railroad tracks lights flashed, green,
red . . . Varya stopped and, as she looked at the
lights, began to quote:

A Visit to Friends

Straight is the railroad: the narrow embankments,
The milestones, bridges and rails,
And to either side, everywhere, lie Russian bones . . .
How many there are! * . . .

"How does it go on? Oh, good lord, I've forgotten
everything!"

We have worn ourselves out in the heat, in the cold,
With backs everlastingly stooped . . .

She recited in a splendid deep voice, with feeling;
a lively blush lit up her face, and tears came to her
eyes. Here was the old Varya, Varya the college girl,
and as he listened to her, Podgorin thought of the
past and remembered how he himself, when a student, knew many fine poems by heart and loved to recite them.

His bent back he has never straightened
To this very day: dull and silent . . .

But Varya could not remember any more . . . She
fell silent and smiled weakly and listlessly, and after
her recitation the green and red lights took on a mournful aspect.
"Oh, I've forgotten it!"
Podgorin, however, had suddenly remembered it,
as though it had accidentally survived in his memory

* "The Railroad," a poem by Nikolai Alexeyevich Nekrasov
(1821–1877).

[160]

from his student years, and he recited softly, in a low tone:

The people of Russia have borne enough,
And the railroad, too, they will bear,—
They will suffer it all—and a broad, shining path
They will carve for themselves with their breasts . . .
'Tis only a pity . . .

" ' 'Tis only a pity,' " Varya interrupted him, having remembered it. " ' 'Tis only a pity neither thou nor I will live in that marvelous age!' "

And she suddenly laughed and clapped him on the shoulder.

They returned to the house and sat down to supper. Sergei Sergeyich tucked the corner of his napkin carelessly into his collar in imitation of someone or other.

"Let's have a drink," he said, pouring out vodka for himself and Podgorin. "We old students knew how to drink and how to talk and how to do our work. I drink your health, my old friend, and you shall drink the health of an old fool of an idealist and wish that he may die an idealist. Only the grave can cure a hunchback."

Tatyana looked tenderly at her husband all through supper, jealous and uneasy lest he should eat or drink something bad for him. It seemed to her that he had been spoiled by women, that he was tired—she liked this in him, but at the same time she suffered. Varya and Nadya were also tender with Sergei and looked at him anxiously, as if they were afraid he would suddenly take off and leave them. When he wished to pour himself a second drink, Varya put on a stern face and said:

"You are poisoning yourself, Sergei Sergeyich. You are a highly strung, sensitive person and it would be easy for you to become an alcoholic. Tanya, have them take the vodka away."

Sergei Sergeyich generally had great success with women. They loved his height, his build, his big features, his indolence and his misfortunes. They said that he was very goodhearted, and that was why he was a spendthrift; that he was an idealist and therefore impractical; that he was an honest, pure soul unable to adapt himself to people and circumstances, and that was why he owned nothing and could not find himself any definite work. They trusted him implicitly, worshiped him and spoiled him with their adoration, until he himself began to believe that he was an idealist, an impractical, honest, pure soul, and in every way higher and better than these women.

"Why haven't you complimented my little girls?" said Tatyana, looking lovingly at her two healthy, well-fed little daughters who resembled two butter balls, as she set before them dishes filled with rice. "Just look at them! They say all mothers praise their children, but I assure you, I am not biased—my little girls *are* extraordinary. Especially the elder one."

Podgorin smiled at her and at the little girls, but it seemed strange to him that this young, healthy, sensible woman, such a great, complex organism, should be spending all her energy and all her strength on such a simple, small task as the organization of this nest, which was quite well enough organized as it was.

Perhaps this is the way things have to be, he thought, but it is uninteresting and unintelligent.

" 'Before he could gasp, he was in the bear's clasp,*' " said Sergei Sergeyich, quoting Krilov's fable, and snapped his fingers.

They finished supper. Tatyana and Varya made Podgorin sit down on a couch in the drawing room and began talking to him about business again, in undertones.

"We must save Sergei Sergeyich," said Varya, "it is our moral duty. He has his weaknesses, he is improvident, he doesn't think of preparing for a rainy day, but it's all because he is so kind and generous. He has the soul of a child. If you gave him a million, in a month he would have nothing left. He would have given it all away."

---

* From Krilov's well-known fable, "The Peasant and the Farmhand" (in which a man goes out to catch a bear and the bear catches him).

"It's true, it's true," said Tatyana, and tears ran down her cheeks. "I have suffered a great deal for him, but I must admit he's a wonderful man."

And neither Tatyana nor Varya could refrain from a little stroke of cruelty in reproaching Podgorin, "But your generation is no longer like that, Misha!"

What has this got to do with generations? thought Podgorin. Losev is only six years older than I, no more . . .

"It's not easy to live in this world," said Varya and sighed. "A man is continually threatened by some loss or other. Either they want to take your estate away from you, or one of your dear ones becomes sick and you are afraid he will die—and so it goes day after day. But what is one to do, my friends? We must submit to the will of the Almighty without complaining; we must remember that nothing in this world happens by chance, that everything has its remote purpose. You've had very little experience of life yet, Misha. You've suffered very little and you will laugh at me; go ahead and laugh, I will say it anyway—just when I was the most consumed with anxiety I have had several instances of clairvoyance, and this has caused a revolution in my soul and now I know that nothing happens by chance, that everything that happens in our lives is necessary."

This Varya, already gray, laced up in a corset, wearing a fashionable dress with short puffed sleeves,

Varya twisting a cigarette in her long thin fingers, which for some reason were trembling, Varya lightly falling into mysticism, speaking so listlessly and monotonously—how different was this Varya from Varya the college girl, red-headed, gay, noisy, daring . . .

And where has it all disappeared to! thought Podgorin, listening to her with boredom.

"Sing something, Va," he said, to bring this talk about clairvoyance to an end. "You used to sing very well once."

"Oh, Misha, those days are gone."

"All right, then recite something from Nekrasov."

"I've forgotten it all. That thing came to me earlier by accident."

In spite of the corset and the short sleeves, it was plain that she was hard up and half-starving in her factory near Tula. And it was very plain that she was overworked; her hard, monotonous labor, together with her eternal interference in the affairs of others and her anxiety for her friends had tired and aged her, so that Podgorin, as he looked at her faded, sorrowful face, thought that actually it was not Kuzminky nor Sergei Sergeyich, whose cause she was pleading, who should be helped, but she herself.

It seemed that higher education and the fact that she had become a physician had not affected her as a woman. Just like Tatyana she loved weddings, births, christenings and long talks about children; she loved scary novels with happy endings, and read the papers only for the fires, floods and ceremonial festivals; she badly wanted Podgorin to propose to Nadezhda, and would have burst into tears of joy if this had come about.

He did not know whether it happened by chance or whether Varya had arranged it, but he found himself alone with Nadezhda. Yet the very suspicion that they were watching him and wanted something from him embarrassed and disturbed him, and he felt, beside Nadezhda, as though they had been put in one cage together.

"Let's go into the garden," she said.

They went into the garden; he—reluctantly, with a feeling of annoyance, not knowing what to talk to her about, and she—happy and proud to be near him, obviously pleased that he was going to stay another three days here, and filled, probably, with sweet dreams and hopes. He did not know whether or not she loved him, but he did know that she had grown used to him and attached to him a long time ago and still saw him as her teacher, and that her heart was filled now with the same emotions that had moved her sister Tatyana years ago; that is, she now thought of nothing but love, of being married very soon and having a husband, children and a home of her own. She had retained to this day that feeling of close friendship which is sometimes so strong in children, and it was very likely that she only respected Podgorin and loved him as a friend, having fallen in love not with him, but with these very dreams of a husband and children.

"It's beginning to get dark," he said.

"Yes. The moon rises late now."

They were walking all the time along a single pathway near the house. Podgorin did not wish to go into the depths of the garden; it was so dark there he would have to take Nadezhda by the arm, be very close to her. Shadows were moving on the terrace, and it seemed to him that Tatyana and Varya were watching him.

"I must ask your advice," said Nadezhda, coming to a halt. "If Kuzminky is sold, then Sergei Sergeyich will go into government service and our life will be completely changed. I shan't go with my sister; we shall part, because I don't want to be a burden to her family. I shall have to work. I'll get a job somewhere in Moscow—earn a salary and help my sister and her husband. You will help me with your advice, won't you?"

Completely unaccustomed to work, she was now inspired by the idea of an independent life; she was making plans for the future—it was written in her face—and this life, when she would be working and helping others, seemed wonderful and poetic to her. He saw her pale face and dark eyebrows very close to him and remembered what an intelligent, quick-witted student she had been, how full of promise, and how pleasant it had been to give her lessons. Here, probably, was no ordinary young woman who wished for a husband, but an intelligent, noble girl, extraordinarily kind, with a gentle, soft heart, out of whom, as from wax, one could mold anything one wished, and who would grow into a superb woman, once given the right surroundings.

Really, why shouldn't I marry her? thought Podgorin, but immediately, for some reason, he was frightened by the thought and went back to the house.

Tatyana was sitting at the grand piano in the drawing room, and her playing vividly recalled the past, when in this very drawing room they would play, sing and dance until the small hours, with the windows flung wide, and the birds in the garden and by the river would be singing too. Podgorin cheered up, began to fool around, danced with Nadezhda and Varya and afterward sang. A corn on his foot bothered him and he asked permission to put on Sergei Sergeyich's slippers; strange to say, in the slippers he began to feel really one of the family—Just like a brother-in-law, flashed into his mind—and he became still happier. As they looked at him they all revived and cheered up, as though they had grown younger. Their faces began to glow with hope: Kuzminky would be saved! Really it was so simple; someone had only to think up something, to dip into the law books or to marry off Nadya to Podgorin . . . And obviously things were already moving forward. Nadya, rosy and happy, her eyes full of tears in anticipation of something quite out of the ordinary, whirled in the dance, her white dress billowing out and revealing her lovely slender legs in flesh-colored stockings . . . Varya, very pleased, took Podgorin by the arm and said to him in a low voice with a meaningful expression:

"Misha, don't run away from your happiness. Take hold of it when it puts itself in your hands, for afterward, even though you may chase after it, it will be too late—you will not catch up with it."

Podgorin felt like making promises and encouraging hopes, and by now he even believed, himself, that Kuzminky could be saved and that it was a simple thing to do.

" 'And you will be-e-e-e the queen of the wo-o-o-orld,*' " he began to sing, adopting a pose, and then all at once he remembered that nothing could be done for these people, absolutely nothing, and he grew quiet like a guilty person.

Afterward he sat silently in a corner, with his feet, in the borrowed slippers, crossed under him.

As they looked at him the rest of them understood, too, that nothing could be done, and they became very quiet. They closed the piano. Everyone remarked that

* "The Demon," Part II, by Mikhail Yurievich Lermontov (1814–1841).

it was already late, that it was time to go to bed, and Tatyana put out the big lamp in the drawing room.

A bed had been prepared for Podgorin in the same wing where he had lived long ago. Sergei Sergeyich went along to lead the way, holding the candle high above his head, although by now the moon was coming up and it was light. They walked along the avenue between the lilac bushes, and the gravel rustled under their feet.

" 'Before he could gasp, he was in the bear's clasp,' " said Sergei Sergeyich.

It seemed to Podgorin that he had heard this phrase a thousand times by now. He was sick of it! When they reached the wing, Sergei Sergeyich pulled out of his roomy jacket a bottle and two glasses and set them on the table.

"It's cognac," he said. "Five star. It's impossible to take a drink with Varya in the house, she starts off at once about alcoholism; but here we're free. It's splendid cognac."

They sat down. The cognac indeed turned out to be excellent.

"Let's drink hearty today," went on Sergei Sergeyich, chewing on slices of lemon between drinks. "I'm the old student type, I like to have fun once in a while. One needs it!"

But there was the same look in his eyes, as if he

needed something from Podgorin and was on the
point of asking him for it.

"Let's drink up, old fellow," he went on with a sigh.
"Things have turned out so badly I have to take it.
For us old eccentrics the end has come, the roof has
fallen in. Idealism is not in vogue now. The ruble is
king now, and if you don't want to be pushed out
of the way, you must fling yourself down before the
ruble and grovel. I can't do it. It's sickening!"

"When is the sale arranged for?" asked Podgorin,
to change the subject.

"The seventh of August. But I'm not counting on
saving Kuzminky, my dear. There's a tremendous pile
of arrears and the estate doesn't bring in any income,
only losses every year. It's not worth it . . . Tanya is
sorry, of course, it's her ancestral home, but I admit
I am even glad in a way. I'm not cut out for village
life at all. My sphere is the great, noisy city; my element, the fight!"

He went on talking, but still without saying what he
wanted, and he watched Podgorin closely as though
only waiting for an opportune moment. And suddenly
Podgorin saw his eyes very near, felt his breath on his
face . . .

"Save me, my dear!" Sergei Sergeyich muttered,
breathing heavily. "Give me two hundred rubles! I
beg of you!"

Podgorin felt like saying that he was pressed for money himself, and he reflected that it would be better to give those two hundred rubles to some poor man or even to lose it at cards; but he was terribly embarrassed and, feeling as though he were in a trap in this tiny room with its single candle, and wanting to rid himself quickly of that breathing, of those soft hands that clasped him round the waist and already seemed to be sticking to him, he began quickly looking in his pockets for his notebook, where his money was.

"Here . . ." he muttered, taking out a hundred rubles. "You will get the rest later. I have no more on me. You see, I can't say no," he added with irritation, beginning to get angry. "I have an impossible character, like an old woman's. Only do pay me back later, please. I'm hard up myself."

"Thank you. *Thank* you, old man!"

"And for God's sake stop fancying yourself as an idealist. If you're an idealist, I'm a turkey. You're just an irresponsible loafer and nothing else."

Sergei Sergeyich sighed deeply and sat down on the sofa.

"My dear, you are angry with me," he said, "but if you only knew how wretched I am! I'm going through a horrible time just now. I swear, my dear, it's not myself I'm sorry for, no! I'm sorry for my wife and children. If it weren't for my children and my wife, I would have done away with myself long ago."

And suddenly his head and shoulders began to shake, and he burst into sobs.

"That would be the last straw," said Podgorin, walking agitatedly up and down the room and feeling intensely annoyed. "What on earth can one do with a man who has caused a great deal of harm and then sobs about it? Your tears disarm me, I haven't the heart to say anything to you. You are sobbing . . . that means you must be in the right."

"*I* have caused a great deal of harm?" asked Sergei Sergeyich, standing up and looking at Podgorin in astonishment. "Dear man, how can you say that? *I* have caused a lot of harm? Oh, how little you know me! How little you understand me!"

"Fine, maybe I don't understand you. Only, please, don't sob. It's disgusting."

"Oh, how little you know me!" repeated Losev, with perfect sincerity. "How little you know me!"

"Take a look at yourself in the glass," went on Podgorin. "You're no longer a young man, you will soon be old. It's time to take stock of yourself, to realize something, at least, of who you are and what you are. Your whole life spent doing nothing, your whole life given over to this idle, childish chattering, clowning, putting on airs—isn't your own head spinning, aren't you fed up with living this way, really? I'm sick of you! Bored to death with you!"

[173]

After he had said this Podgorin left the wing and slammed the door. For almost the first time in his life he had been candid and said what he wanted to.

A few moments later he was already sorry that he had been so harsh. What was the good of speaking seriously or arguing with a man who continually lied, ate too much, drank too much, wasted other people's money and at the same time was convinced that he was an idealist and a sufferer? It all sprang from foolishness or from old bad habits which were strongly entrenched in the organism, like a disease, and by now incurable. In any case, indignation and harsh reproaches were no use here, and it would be better to laugh at him; one good sneer would do far more than a dozen sermons!

It would be simpler not to pay the matter any attention at all, Podgorin thought, but the main thing is, not to give him any money.

But a moment later he was no longer thinking of Sergei Sergeyich or his hundred rubles. It was a night made for dreaming, quiet and very bright. When Podgorin looked up at the sky on moonlight nights, it seemed to him that only he and the moon were awake, everything else was asleep or drowsing; and he stopped thinking about people and money, and little by little his spirit grew quiet and tranquil; he felt himself all alone in the world, and in the silence of the night the sound of his own footsteps seemed to him full of sadness.

The garden was enclosed by a white stone wall. On the side leading into the open country, in the right-hand corner, stood a watch tower. The lower part of it was stone but the top was wooden, with a little platform, a conical roof and a tall steeple on which a weathercock stood out darkly. Downstairs were two doors, through which one could pass from the garden into the fields; a stairway that squeaked under one's feet led up to the platform from below. Under the stairs was a pile of old broken-down armchairs, and the light of the moon entering now through the doorway was shining on these chairs, and with their crooked broken legs sticking up in the air they seemed to have come to life in the night and to be lying in wait for someone in the stillness.

Podgorin climbed the stairs to the platform and sat down. Immediately beyond the wall was the boundary ditch with a bank, and beyond that lay the open fields, stretching far and wide, flooded with moonlight. Podgorin knew that the forest lay directly before him, three versts from the estate, and now it seemed to him he could see a dark line in the distance. Quail and corncrakes were crying, and now and again from the edge of the forest came the call of a cuckoo that was also awake.

A dog began barking. Someone was coming across the garden, drawing near the tower.

"Zhuk!" a woman's voice called softly. "Zhuk, come back!"

Below, Podgorin could hear the footsteps of someone entering the tower, and a moment later a black dog, an old friend of Podgorin's, appeared on the bank. It stopped, looked up at the place where Podgorin was sitting and began wagging its tail in a friendly way. A few moments later a white figure arose out of the black ditch like a shadow and also stopped on the bank. It was Nadezhda.

"What do you see there?" she asked the dog, and began looking intently upward.

She did not see Podgorin but probably she sensed his nearness for she was smiling, and her pale face, illumined by the moon, looked happy. The black shadow of the tower, stretching along the ground far into the fields, the motionless white figure with the blissful smile on its pale face, the black dog, their two shadows—all of it together was like a dream . . .

"There is someone there," Nadezhda murmured softly.

She stood there waiting for him to come down or to call her up to him and at last declare himself, so that they could both be happy on this quiet, glorious night. White, wan, slender and very beautiful in the moonlight, she was expecting tenderness; her constant dreams of happiness and love had exhausted her, and by now it was beyond her power to conceal her feelings; her whole figure, the brilliance of her eyes and her fixed happy smile betrayed her secret thoughts. As for him, he felt uncomfortable, he shrank into himself and was quiet, and did not know whether to speak up and pass it all off as a joke, as usual, or to keep silent; he was annoyed with himself and could only think that here in this country estate, on a moonlight night, beside a beautiful girl in love and dreaming, he was as unmoved as on his visits to Malaya Bronnaya Street, because evidently all this poetry had lost its meaning for him just as the coarse prose had. And there was no longer any meaning for him either in moonlight meetings, or in slim-waisted white figures, or in mysterious shadows, or in watchtowers and country estates, or in such 'types' as Sergei Sergeyich, or in the kind of people such as he, Podgorin, had himself become, with his cold boredom, his eternal discontent, his inability to adjust to real life and to take what it offered him, and his painful, aching hunger for what did not and could not exist on earth. And as he sat there in the tower, he felt he would have much preferred to see a display of fireworks, or some procession or other under the moonlight, or hear Varya again reciting "The Railroad"; or he would have preferred another woman to stand there on the bank, where Nadezhda was standing now, and speak about something interesting and new, having nothing to do with love or happiness. Yet at the same time if she *were* to speak of love, it would be to call for a new form of life, lofty and intelligent, on the eve of which we are perhaps already living, and of which we have a presentiment now and again.

"There is no one there," said Nadezhda.

And after waiting another minute, she walked away in the direction of the forest, in silence, her head drooping. The dog ran on in front of her. Podgorin could see the little patch of white for a long time afterward.

Strange, how it all came out! he kept thinking to himself as he made his way back to his room in the wing.

He could not imagine what he could say to Sergei Sergeyich or to Tatyana, or how he was to behave toward Nadezhda tomorrow, and the day after tomorrow too—and he began to suffer the embarrassment, fear and boredom in advance. How was he to fill in those long three days he had promised to spend here? He remembered the conversation about clairvoyance and Sergei Sergeyich's phrase: "Before he could gasp, he was in the bear's clasp"; he remembered that tomorrow, to please Tatyana, he would have to smile at her well-fed, plump little girls—and he decided to leave.

At half-past six Sergei Sergeyich appeared on the terrace of the big house in a Bokharan dressing gown and a fez with a tassel. Podgorin, without wasting a minute, walked over to him and began to say goodbye.

"I have to be in Moscow at ten o'clock," he said, not meeting the other's eyes. "I had completely forgotten they will be expecting me at the notary's office. You must please excuse me. When your family gets up, please give them my apologies, I'm terribly sorry . . ."

He did not hear what Sergei Sergeyich said to him and hurried away, looking back over his shoulder at the windows of the big house all the time, afraid lest the ladies should wake up and detain him. He was ashamed of his nervousness. He felt that he was seeing Kuzminky for the last time, and that he would never come back here again; and as he was leaving he glanced back several times at the wing where he had once passed so many happy days, but his heart was cold; he felt no sorrow.

At home the first thing he noticed was the note he had read yesterday, lying on the desk. "My dear Misha," he read, "You have utterly forgotten us; do come and pay us a visit right away . . ."

And for no reason he recalled how Nadezhda had whirled in the dance, and how her dress had billowed out, revealing her legs in flesh-colored stockings . . .

Ten minutes later he was already sitting at his desk, working, and no longer thinking about Kuzminky at all.

A Reward Denied

An unfinished short story

⌈1902-1903⌉

They were holding a service of evening prayer in the house of Mikhail Ilyich Bondarev, the district Marshal of Nobility. A young priest, a plump blond youth with long curls and a broad nose like a lion's, was officiating. Only the deacon and the clerk were chanting.

Mikhail Ilyich, who was seriously ill, sat motionless in an armchair, pale, with closed eyes, almost like a corpse. His wife Vera Andreyevna stood beside him, her head inclined to one side, in the relaxed, submissive attitude of one who is indifferent to religion, yet obliged to stand and to make the sign of the cross from time to time. Vera Andreyevna's brother, Alexander Andreyich Yanshin, and his wife Lenochka were standing behind the armchair and also alongside. It was Whitsun eve. The trees were whispering quietly in the garden, and a glorious evening sunset blazed as though for a festival, covering half the sky.

Whether the sound of bells from the town or the monastery chimes were heard through the open window, or a peacock screaming from the courtyard, or someone coughing in the vestibule, the same thought passed unbidden through everyone's mind: that Mikhail Ilyich was seriously ill, that the doctors had ordered him to be taken abroad as soon as his health improved even slightly, but that from day to day he grew now better, now worse; that no one could make anything of it, and that meanwhile time was passing and the uncertainty was tiresome. Yanshin had arrived at Eastertime intending to help his sister take her husband abroad; yet he was still living here with his wife after nearly two months, and this was the third evening service he had attended already; the future was still in a fog and no one could make anything of it. No one could even guarantee that this nightmare would not drag on until the autumn.

Yanshin was discontented and bored. He was tired of getting ready to go abroad every day, and by now he wanted to go home to his own place in Novoselki. True, there was no gaiety at home either, but on the other hand there was no enormous hall there with a column in each corner, no white armchairs with gilt upholstery, yellow curtains, chandeliers and all this bourgeois tastelessness aspiring to magnificence, no echoes resounding after every footstep in the night, and above all—there was no sickly, yellow, podgy face with closed eyes. At home he could laugh, talk foolishly, quarrel noisily with his wife or his mother, in a word—live as he pleased; but here, just as in a boarding school, one had to walk on tip-toe, whisper, talk only sense, or stand here, and listen to the evening prayer, which was being held not out of any religious feeling but, as Mikhail Ilyich himself said, in accordance with tradition . . . And nothing is as tiring and humiliating as having to humble yourself before a man whom in the depths of your heart you consider a nonentity, and to fuss over a sick man for whom you are not sorry . . .

Yanshin was thinking of another particular matter: last night his wife Lenochka had told him she was pregnant. This news was of interest only because it brought a new anxiety to the question of their trip. What should he do? Should he take Lenochka abroad with him, or send her back to his mother in Novoselki? For it would be awkward traveling in her condition, yet she would on no account go home, for she did not get on with her mother-in-law and would never consent to live in the country alone, without her husband.

Or should I take advantage of the excuse and go home with her? thought Yanshin, trying not to listen to the deacon. No, it would be awkward leaving Vera here alone . . . he decided, glancing quickly at his sister's shapely figure. But what am I to do?

He pondered, asking himself, "What am I to do?" and his life seemed to him extremely complicated and tangled. All the problems involving the journey, his sister, his wife, his brother-in-law, and so on—each one, taken alone, could probably be solved easily and conveniently; but they were all tangled up together and resembled a deep morass, and if any one of his problems were to be solved, all the others would be only the more tangled up.

When, before beginning to read the gospel, the priest turned round and said, "Peace be unto you all!" the invalid Mikhail Ilyich suddenly opened his eyes and stirred in his armchair.

"Sasha!" he called.

Yanshin went up to him quickly and bent down.

"I don't like the way he is conducting the service . . ." said Mikhail Ilyich in a low voice, but one that carried his words clearly through the room; his breathing came heavily, with whistling and wheezing. "I should like to leave. Help me out, Sasha."

Yanshin helped him to stand up and took him by the arm.

"You stay here, dear . . ." said Mikhail Ilyich in a weak supplicating voice to his wife, who wished to take him by the other arm. "Stay here!" he repeated with irritation, as he glanced at her indifferent face. "I can get there like this!"

The priest stood with the open gospel and waited. In the silence that followed, the harmonious singing of a chorus of men's voices could be clearly heard. They were singing somewhere beyond the garden, perhaps down by the river. And the effect was lovely when the bells in the nearby monastery suddenly began to ring and their soft, melodious sound mingled with the singing. Yanshin's heart was wrung by sweet presentiments of something wonderful, and he almost forgot that he had to lead the invalid. The sounds floating into the hall from outdoors reminded him, for some reason, how little delight and freedom there was in his present life and how petty, worthless and dull were the problems whose solution he was pursuing so strenuously from dusk to dawn each day. When he led the sick man out and the servants, drawing aside to make room for them, stared with that gloomy curiosity with which country people habitually look at a corpse, Yanshin felt a sudden hatred, an intense sharp hatred, for the sick man's podgy, clean-shaven actor's face, for his hands with their waxen color, for his velvet dressing gown and his breathing and the tapping of his black cane. This feeling, which he had never experienced in his whole life before, overwhelmed him quite unexpectedly and made him go cold from head to foot; his heart began to beat fast. He passionately wanted Michail Ilyich to die that very minute, to cry out for the last time and collapse onto the floor; but in a moment he had a vision of that death and drew back from it in horror . . . When they had left the hall, he no longer desired the invalid's death but only life for himself; he wanted to tear his hands away from this warm armpit and flee, flee, flee without a backward glance.

A bed had been prepared for Mikhail Ilyich on a Turkish divan in his study. In his bedroom the sick man seemed hot and uncomfortable.

"Be one thing or the other: either a priest or a hussar!" he said as he sank down heavily onto the divan. "What manners! Oh, my God . . . I'd have a dandified priest like that one demoted to sexton."

As he looked at the petulant, miserable face, Yanshin felt like making a retort, saying something impudent, revealing his hatred, but he remembered the doctor's orders not to vex the patient and he kept silent. However, it was not on the doctor's account. What would he not have said, or shouted aloud, if his sister Vera had not been tied forever and hopelessly to this despicable man? Mikhail Ilyich had a way of constantly sticking out his compressed lips and moving them from side to side as though sucking on a fruit-drop, and this motion of the thick, clean-shaven lips was irritating Yanshin now.

"You go back there, Sasha," said Mikhail Ilyich. "You are a healthy man and indifferent to the Church, apparently . . . For you it is all the same, whoever conducts the service. Go."

"But you are indifferent to the Church too, you

know . . ." said Yanshin quietly, restraining himself.

"No, I believe in Providence and I acknowledge the Church."

"Exactly. As I see it, you don't need God or truth in your religion, only words like 'providence' and 'from on high' . . ."

Yanshin felt like adding, "Otherwise you could not have insulted the priest as you did today," but he did not say it. It seemed to him that he had already allowed himself to say too much as it was.

"Please go back!" said Mikhail Ilyich impatiently, for he did not like it when people disagreed with him or talked about him. "I don't want to be a burden to anyone . . . I know how wearisome it is to sit beside an invalid . . . I know, old man. I have always said and I always will say, there is no labor harder or holier than the labor of the sick-nurse. Do me a favor and go."

Yanshin left the study. When he had gone downstairs to his own room, he put on his hat and coat and went out through the front door into the garden. It was now almost nine o'clock. They were singing hymns upstairs. As he made his way among the flower-beds, the rose bushes, the pale blue monogram V and M—for Vera and Mikhail—composed in heliotrope, and passed by a great number of wonderful flowers which gave pleasure to no one on this estate but grew and blossomed, probably, also 'in accordance with tradition,' Yanshin hurried, afraid lest his wife should call to him from upstairs. She could see him easily. But now, after going some distance through the park, he had reached a long dark avenue of firs, through which in the evening one could sometimes see the sunset. Here a light, ominous whispering would come from the old, decrepit fir trees even in still weather; there was a smell of resin, and one's feet slipped on the dry needles.

As he walked, Yanshin was thinking about that hatred which had so unexpectedly overwhelmed him today at the time of the evening prayers, which had not left him even yet and which he would have to reckon with; it had brought yet another complication into his life and promised little good. But from the fir trees, the quiet, distant sky and the festive sunset there breathed forth an air of peace and heavenly bliss. He listened with delight to his own footsteps which rang out lonely and hollow in the dark avenue, and he stopped asking himself, "What am I to do?"

He used to walk to the station almost every evening to get the papers and letters, and while he was living at his brother-in-law's it was his only diversion. The mail-train came through at a quarter to ten, at exactly the time when the unbearable evening tedium was setting in at the house. There was no one to play cards with, there was no late supper, he did not feel like going to bed, and therefore against his will he found himself either sitting with the sick man or reading aloud to Lenochka from the translated foreign novels that she loved. The station was large, with a refreshment room and a bookstall. One could have a snack or a drink of beer and look through the books. But better than anything else Yanshin enjoyed meeting the train and envying the passengers, who were on their way somewhere and, it seemed to him, happier than he was.

When he got to the station, that public he was used to seeing there every evening was already milling about the platform waiting for the train. Here were the "summer people" who lived near the station, two or three officers from town, and a country gentleman with a spur on his right foot and a Great Dane walking behind him with mournfully lowered head. The summer people, both men and women, obviously knew one another well, and were laughing and talking loudly. Livelier than them all, as usual, and laughing loudest of all was a vacationing engineer, a very fat man of about forty-five, with side whiskers and a broad posterior, dressed in a calico overblouse and wide velveteen trousers. When he walked past Yanshin, thrusting his big stomach out in front, stroking his whiskers and glancing cordially at him with his oily eyes, he struck Yanshin as a man with a great appetite for life. There was usually a particular expression on the engineer's face which it was impossible to read otherwise than: 'Ah, how tasty!' His family name was a clumsy, three-worded one and Yanshin remembered it only because the engineer, who loved to argue and talk loudly about politics, would often utter an oath and say,

"Else I'm not Bitny-Kushla-Suvremovich!"

He was said to be a very jolly man, wonderfully hospitable and a passionate whist player. Yanshin had wanted to get to know him for a long time but he could not bring himself to go up to him and start a conversation, although he guessed that he would have no objection to the acquaintance. Strolling alone along the platform and listening to the summer people, Yanshin for some reason would remember each time that he was thirty-one years old and that, beginning with his twenty-fourth year when he graduated from the university, he had not had a single really enjoyable day: either he had a lawsuit with his neighbor over their boundary line, or his wife had a miscarriage, or his sister Vera seemed to be miserable, or now Mikhail Ilyich was ill and it had become necessary to take him abroad. He reflected that all this would go on and be repeated in different ways endlessly, and that at forty and fifty he would have the same anxieties and thoughts as at thirty-one—that, in a word, he would never escape from this hard shell until his very death. To think otherwise, one must be able to deceive oneself. And he longed to stop being an oyster, even if only for an hour; he longed to get a glimpse into someone else's life, to be enthralled by something quite outside his personal life, to talk to people who were completely strange to him, even perhaps to this fat engineer or to the summer women, who in the evening twilight were all so lovely, happy and above all—young.

The train came in. The country gentleman with the single spur went to meet a stout, elderly lady who embraced him and repeated several times in a voice filled with emotion *"Alexis!"* In all probability, it was his mother. Ceremoniously, like a *jeune premier* in the ballet, he tinkled his spur, took her arm and said to the porter in a velvety, honeyed baritone, "Be so kind as to get our baggage!"

The train left very soon. The summer people had got their papers and letters and set out for their homes. Silence closed in . . . Yanshin strolled up and down the platform a little while longer and went into the first-class waiting room. He did not feel hungry, but nevertheless he ate a helping of veal and drank some beer. The ceremonious, refined manners of the country gentleman with the spur, his honeyed baritone and his politeness in which there was so little of simplicity had made an inescapable, painful impression on him. He remembered his long mustaches, his kind and rather sensible, yet somehow strange and incomprehensible face, his way of rubbing his hands as though he were cold, and he thought that if the stout, elderly lady were indeed the mother of this man, then she was probably very unhappy. Her emotional voice had spoken only one word, *"Alexis!"*, but her timid, perplexed face and loving eyes had filled in all the rest.

Through the window Vera Andreyevna saw her brother go out. She knew he was going to the station and she conjured up to herself the avenue of firs all the way to the very end, then the slope down to the river, the wide view and that impression of peace and simplicity that rivers and water meadows always made upon her; and farther on the railway station and the birch forest where the summer people lived, and far off to the right the little town of the district and the monastery with its golden cupolas . . . Afterwards she again pictured to herself the avenue, the darkness, her fear and shame, the well-known footsteps, and everything which might happen all over again, perhaps even today . . . She left the room for a minute to see that they had ordered tea served to the priest, and as she entered the dining room she took from her pocket a letter in a stiff envelope with a foreign postmark, folded double. This letter had been brought to her five minutes before the evening prayers, and she had already found time to read it twice.

A Reward Denied

MY DARLING, DEAREST, MY TORMENT, AND MY LONGING, she read, holding the letter in both hands so that they might both feast on the touch of those sweet, ardent lines.

MY DARLING, she began again from the first words, DEAREST, MY TORMENT, AND MY LONGING, you write most convincingly, but all the same I don't know what I should do. You said then that you would *certainly* be going to Italy, and I, like a madman, rushed ahead to meet you here and to love my darling, my joy. I thought that here you would no longer be afraid of the moonlight nights lest your husband or your brother should see my shadow from the window. Here I could stroll with you along the streets, and you would not be afraid of Rome or Venice finding out that we loved each other. Forgive me, my treasure, but there is one Vera who is timid, easily frightened and vacillating, and there is another Vera—indifferent, cold, proud, who in front of strangers calls me "you" and pretends she hardly notices me. I want this other one, this proud and beautiful one, to love me . . . I don't want to be an owl who is only allowed to enjoy itself in the evening and the night. Give me light! The darkness depresses me, my darling, and this snatched and furtive love of ours keeps me half-starved and I am out of temper, I suffer, it is driving me mad . . . Well, in short, I thought that my Vera, not the first one but the second, here, in a foreign country, where it is easier to escape from surveillance than at home, would perhaps grant me one hour of complete, genuine love, without a backward glance, so that at least once, as it should be, I could feel like a lover instead of a smuggler, so that when you are in my arms you wouldn't say, "It's time for me to go!" This is what I thought, but a whole month has gone by since I came to live in Florence; you are not here, and

[195]

nothing is definite. You write: "We can hardly manage to get away this month." What does this mean? My despair, what are you doing to me!? You must realize I can't live without you, I can't, I can't!!! They say Italy is glorious, but to me it is as dreadfully tedious here as in any exile, and, like an exile, my impassioned love grows more and more impatient. You will say my pun is not funny, but *I* am funny, to make up for it, like a jester. I dash about, from Bologna to Venice to Rome, and I look everywhere in the throngs of women for one who looks like you. Out of boredom I have already made the rounds of all the art galleries and museums five times, and in the pictures I see only you alone. In Rome I have climbed Mount Pincio, rather out of breath, and looked down upon the Eternal City, but the eternity, the beauty and the sky—they all blend together into a single vision with your face and your dress. And here, in Florence, I go into the shops where they sell sculpture and when there is no one about in the shop, I put my arms round the statues and it seems to me I am putting my arms round you. I need you instantly, this very minute . . . Vera, I am going out of my mind; but forgive me, I can't help myself, I am leaving tomorrow to return to you . . . This letter is superfluous. All right, let it be superfluous! It means I have decided, my darling. I am leaving tomorrow.

The Fiancée

[1903]

It was now about ten o'clock at night, and a full moon was shining on the garden. At the home of the Shumins, the evening prayers that grandmother Marfa Mikhailovna had ordered were just over, and now Nadya—she had gone out into the garden for a minute—could see the table in the big hall being set for supper and her grandmother bustling about the room in her luxurious silk gown. Father Andrei, the archpriest of the diocese, was talking something over with Nadya's mother, Nina Ivanovna, who now in the evening light through the window appeared for some reason very young. Nearby stood Father Andrei's son, Andrei Andreyich, listening intently.

In the garden it was cool and quiet, and dark, peaceful shadows lay across the ground. Frogs could be heard croaking as though from somewhere far, very far away, perhaps from the very outskirts of the town. May, the sweet month of May, was in the air everywhere. One breathed deeply, almost believing that somewhere, not here but somewhere under the heavens, above the trees, beyond the city, in the fields and forests, spring had unfolded a life of its own, mysterious, lovely, bountiful and holy, beyond the comprehension of weak, sinful man. And for no reason at all one felt like weeping.

She, Nadya, was now twenty-three years old. Ever since her sixteenth year she had dreamed ardently of marriage, and now at last she was engaged to marry Andrei Andreyich, the man who was standing by the window. She liked him, the wedding was already arranged for the seventh of July, but in spite of this she did not feel happy; she slept badly at night, her gaiety had disappeared . . . Through the open window of the basement, where the kitchen was, came the sound of people scurrying about, the clatter of feet and the banging of the heavy swing door; there was a smell of roast turkey and preserved cherries. And it seemed, somehow, as though her whole life would go on and on as it was now, without change and without end.

Someone came out of the house and stopped on the porch; it was Alexander Timofeyich, or familiarly Sasha, their guest, who had arrived from Moscow about ten days ago. Once, a long time ago, a distant relative of her grandmother's used to come to her for alms—Maria Petrovna, an impoverished widowed gentlewoman, little, thin and sick. She had a son Sasha. He was for some reason spoken of as a fine artist, and when his mother died the old lady, for her soul's salvation, had sent him away to the Komissarov School * in Moscow. In two years he was transferred to the School of Art. He had remained there almost fifteen years, ending up in the faculty of Architecture, where he had just scraped through; he had not gone in for architecture, however, but was working for a Moscow lithographer. He arrived at her grandmother's house almost every summer, usually very sick, to rest and recover his health.

At the moment he wore a buttoned-up frock coat and shabby canvas trousers, frayed at the bottom. His shirt was unpressed and everything about him had an unhealthy look. He was very thin, with big eyes and long, thin fingers, bearded, swarthy and yet handsome for all that. He was as used to the Shumins as if they had been his own family and felt at home with them. Indeed the room in which he lived here had long been known as Sasha's room.

As he stood on the porch, he caught sight of Nadya and went over to her.

"It's lovely here," he said.

"Of course it's lovely. You ought to stay here till autumn."

"Well, it's possible I may have to. Perhaps I shall stay here till September."

* Komissarov School—A technical school in Moscow for art and industry.

He began to laugh for no apparent reason and sat down beside her.

"I'm sitting here looking at Mother," said Nadya. "She looks so young from here! My mother has her faults, of course," she added after a moment's silence, "but still she's a remarkable woman."

"Yes, a fine woman," agreed Sasha. "Your mother is really a very good and a very sweet woman in her own way, but . . . how should I put it? Early this morning I went into your kitchen. There were four women servants sleeping right on the floor, there were no cots, and instead of beds—rags, stench, bedbugs, roaches . . . Exactly the same as it used to be twenty years ago, no change at all. As for your grandmother, God bless her, after all she's an old woman, we have to forgive her; but your mother speaks French, she acts in plays . . . She ought to know better."

When he talked Sasha would stretch out two long, emaciated fingers toward his listener.

"Everything here seems somehow barbarous to me, I'm not used to it," he went on. "The devil knows, no one does a thing! Your mother strolls about all day as though she were a duchess or something, and your grandmother does nothing either, and now you, too. And your fiancée, Andrei Andreyich, he doesn't do a thing either."

Nadya had heard all this last year and, it seemed, the year before. She knew that Sasha was incapable

of arguing in any other way and it had amused her before, but now it annoyed her for some reason.

"This is all old stuff, and I've been tired of it for a
long time," she said and stood up. "If only you would
think up something more original!"

He began to laugh and then he too got up, and they
both walked toward the house. Nadya, tall, beautiful
and graceful, now looked even more healthy and well-
dressed beside him; she felt this and was sorry for him,
and for some reason uncomfortable.

"You talk altogether too much," she said. "Look
how you spoke just now about my Andrei, and you
don't even know him."

"My Andrei . . . Let's forget about him, your
Andrei. It's your own youth I'm sorry for."

When they entered the big room everyone was already sitting down to supper. The grandmother, or
as she was called at home Babulya*, was very fat and
ugly, with heavy eyebrows and a mustache. She
spoke loudly, and it was quite plain from her voice
and manner of speaking that she was the mistress of
this household. She owned a number of stalls at the
market place as well as the old-fashioned house with
its colonnade and garden, but every morning she be-
sought God to save her from ruin, and wept about it
There, too, was her daughter-in-law, Nadya's mother,
Nina Ivanovna, fair-haired, tightly laced, wearing

* *Babulya:* familiar form of *babushka* (grandmother).

[203]

pince-nez, and with diamonds on every finger; and
Father Andrei, too, an old man, lean and toothless,
with the expression of one who is just about to say
something very funny; and his son, Andrei Andreyich,
Nadya's fiancé, stout and handsome, with curly
hair, looking like an actor or a painter. All three of
them were talking about hypnotism.

"You'll be better in a week at my house," said
Babulya, addressing herself to Sasha. "All you need is
a little more to eat. Just look at you!" she sighed.
"You're a dreadful sight! The prodigal son to a tee."

" 'After wasting his substance with riotous living,' "
said Father Andrei slowly, with laughing eyes, " 'the
accursed one would fain have filled his belly with
the husks that the swine did eat.' "

"I love my old dad," said Andrei Andreyich and
touched his father on the shoulder. "He's a fine old
man, a kind old man."

No one said anything. Sasha suddenly burst out
laughing and pressed his napkin to his mouth.

"Then you do believe in hypnotism?" Father
Andrei asked Nina Ivanovna.

"I wouldn't claim to believe in it, of course," Nina
Ivanovna replied, putting on a very serious, even severe expression, "but I must confess that in my opinion there is a great deal in nature that is mysterious
and incomprehensible."

"I'm entirely in agreement with you, only I must

add, for my own part, that faith reduces the area of mystery for us considerably."

They brought in a large, very fat turkey. Father Andrei and Nina Ivanovna went on with their conversation. Nina Ivanovna's diamonds sparkled on her fingers; then tears began to sparkle in her eyes and she became upset.

"Although I wouldn't presume to argue with you," she said, "still, you must agree there are many unsolved riddles in our life!"

"Not a single one, I venture to assure you."

After supper Andrei Andreyich played the violin and Nina Ivanovna accompanied him on the piano. He had taken his university degree in philology ten years ago, but he had never gone into government service and did no definite work of any kind except for taking part occasionally in concerts for charitable causes; so he was referred to in the town as an artiste.

Andrei Andreyich played; they all listened in silence. The samovar bubbled quietly on the table, but Sasha was the only one drinking tea. Afterward, as it struck twelve, a violin string suddenly snapped; everyone laughed and began to bustle about and say good night.

After seeing her fiancé out, Nadya went up to her room on the floor above, where she lived with her mother—her grandmother occupied the lower story. In the hall below they began putting out the lights, but Sasha still sat on drinking tea. He always sat a long time over tea, in the Moscow fashion, drinking as many as seven glasses at a time. Long after she had undressed and gone to bed, Nadya could still hear the servants tidying up downstairs and Babulya grumbling about something. Everything grew quiet at last, and only now and again Sasha's bass voice could be heard coughing in his room downstairs.

When Nadya awoke it was probably about two o'clock; day was just breaking. Somewhere a long way off the nightwatchman's rattle sounded. She did not feel like sleeping, it was uncomfortably soft lying there. As on all the preceding May nights, Nadya sat up in bed and began to think. And her thoughts were all just the same as the night before, monotonous, bothersome, importunate thoughts about how Andrei Andreyich had begun to court her and had proposed to her, how she had accepted him and afterward, little by little, had grown to appreciate this kind, intelligent man. Yet now, for some reason, with no more than a month remaining until the wedding, she began to feel frightened and uneasy, as though something indeterminate and dreadful was awaiting her.

"Click-clack," beat out the nightwatchman lazily. "Click-clack . . . Click-clack. . . ."

Through the big old-fashioned window she can see the garden, the lilac bushes in the distance, thick with flowers, sleepy and limp from the cold. A heavy white mist comes swimming softly toward the lilacs, seeking to cover them up. Sleepy rooks are cawing in the distant trees.

"Oh God, why do I feel so miserable!"

Perhaps every engaged girl feels the same way before her wedding. Who knows? Or was it Sasha's influence? But then Sasha has been saying the same things to her, word for word, for years, and when he said them they always sounded naïve and strange. Then why couldn't she get Sasha out of her head all the same? Why?

The watchman had not been heard for a long time. Under her window and in the garden the birds began to call; the mist lifted from the garden and everything around lit up with the spring light as though with a smile. Soon the whole garden, warm in the sun's embrace, came to life; dewdrops glittered on the leaves like diamonds, and the old, long-neglected garden looked very festive this morning, very young.

Babulya was awake by now. Sasha began coughing in his harsh bass. One could hear people downstairs setting out the samovar and moving the chairs about.

Time passed slowly. Nadya had been up for ages and strolling about the garden for ages and still the morning dragged on.

Along came Nina Ivanovna with a glass of mineral water, her face all tearstained. She had taken up spiritualism and homeopathy, read a great deal and loved to talk about the doubts that plagued her; to Nadya it all seemed to contain a profound mysterious meaning. Now Nadya kissed her mother and walked beside her.

"What were you crying about, Mamma?" she asked.

"Last night I began reading a story about an old man and his daughter. The old man was employed somewhere or other, and his superior fell in love with his daughter. I haven't finished it yet, but there was one place where it was hard to hold back the tears," said Nina Ivanovna and took a sip from her glass. "This morning I remembered it and I cried a little."

"I'm so unhappy all the time lately," said Nadya after a short silence. "Why can't I sleep at night?"

"I really don't know, dear. When I can't sleep at night, I close my eyes very tight, like this, and picture to myself Anna Karenina, walking and talking. Or I imagine some episode from ancient history . . ."

Nadya began to feel that her mother did not understand her and was incapable of understanding her. It was the first time in her life she had had such a feeling and it was quite frightening to her, she wanted to hide; and she went indoors to her room.

At two o'clock they sat down to dine. It was Wednesday, a fast-day, and, therefore, they served the grandmother Lenten borsch and bream with kasha.

To tease the old lady Sasha ate both the meat soup

and the Lenten borsch. He made jokes all the time they were eating, but his jokes were ponderous, they never failed to point a moral, and it was not at all funny when, before making a pun, he would hold up his very long, wasted, almost lifeless fingers and the thought would strike them that he was very ill and unlikely to live in this world much longer; they pitied him then to the point of tears.

After luncheon the old lady went to her room to rest. Nina Ivanovna played the piano a little while, and then she too left.

"Ah, Nadya, my dear," Sasha began his usual afterdinner conversation. "If only you'd listen to me! If only you would!"

She was sitting deep in an old-fashioned armchair, her eyes closed, while he paced the room from one corner to the other.

"If only you would go away and study!" he said. "Only educated and saintly people are of any interest, they alone are of any use. The more there are of people like this, the sooner God's kingdom will come on earth. Bit by bit, not one stone will remain upon another here in this town of yours—everything will be turned upside down, everything will change, as if by magic. And there will be great, magnificent houses here then, wonderful gardens, extraordinary fountains, remarkable people . . . But this is not the main thing. The main thing is that there will be no masses, as we mean the word today, there will be no more of this evil, because each man will have faith and each will know what he is living for, and none will seek support in the mass. My dear, my little darling, go away from here! Show them all you've had enough of this stagnant, humdrum, sinful life. Show it to yourself at least!"

"I can't, Sasha. I'm going to be married."

"Oh rot! What good will that do?"

They went out into the garden and strolled about a little while.

"But be that as it may, my dear, you must grasp, you must realize how unclean, how immoral this idle existence of yours is," Sasha went on. "Try to understand, for instance, that if you and your mother and your babulya do absolutely nothing, it means that someone else is doing your work for you, you are using up someone else's life, and, really, is this decent? Isn't it disgusting?"

Nadya felt like saying "Yes, it's true," she felt like saying that she did understand; but her eyes filled with tears and she suddenly became very quiet, withdrew into herself and went up to her room.

Andrei Andreyich arrived before evening and as usual played the violin for a long time. He was never much of a conversationalist and he was fond of the violin, perhaps, because while he played he did not have to talk. At eleven o'clock, about to go home and already in his overcoat, he embraced Nadya and began greedily kissing her face, her shoulders, her hands.

"My dearest, my sweet, my beautiful one!" he muttered. "Oh, how happy I am! I am out of my mind with joy!"

It seemed to her she had already heard all this long ago, very long ago, or had read it somewhere . . . in some old tattered, long-discarded novel.

Sasha was sitting at the table in the big hall drinking tea, balancing the saucer on his five long fingers; Babulya had laid out a game of patience, Nina Ivanovna was reading. A small flame crackled in the icon lamp, and everything looked peaceful and serene. Nadya said good night, and went upstairs to her room, went to bed and fell asleep at once. But, as on the preceding night, she awoke when the dawn had scarcely broken. She did not feel like sleeping, her heart was troubled and heavy. She sat up, her head leaning on her knees, thinking about her fiancé and about the wedding. For no particular reason she recalled that her mother had not loved her late husband, and now had nothing, but was completely dependent on her mother-in-law, Babulya. Try as she might, Nadya could not understand why until now she had seen something quite special and uncommon in her mother, why she had not observed her to be a simple, ordinary, unhappy woman.

Downstairs Sasha was not asleep either, one could

hear him coughing. He was a strange, naïve person, thought Nadya, and she felt there was something absurd in his visions, in all those wonderful gardens and extraordinary fountains; yet somehow in his naïveté, even in this very absurdity, there was so much that was beautiful that the mere thought of going away to study sent a cold thrill through her whole heart, her whole breast, and she was flooded with a feeling of happiness, of ecstasy.

"I'd better not think about it, better not think about it," she whispered. "I mustn't think about this."

"Click-clack," sounded the nightwatchman somewhere a long way off. "Click-clack . . . click-clack. . . ."

In the middle of June Sasha suddenly grew bored with everything and began to think of returning to Moscow.

"I can't go on living in this town," he said gloomily. "No running water, no sewers. It makes me feel sick to eat at dinner time; the filth in the kitchen is absolutely impossible . . ."

"Do wait a little while, you prodigal son!" Babulya tried to persuade him, whispering for some reason. "The wedding is on the seventh!"

"I don't want to."

"But you were going to stay with us until September, weren't you?"

"Well, I don't want to now. I have work to do."

It happened that the summer was damp and cold, the trees were soggy, everything in the garden looked cheerless and unfriendly. One really did feel like working. Indoors, upstairs and down, unfamiliar women's voices were heard. In the old lady's room the sewing machine rattled away: they were hurrying to finish the trousseau. Nadya was being given six fur coats alone, and the cheapest of them, her grandmother said, cost three hundred rubles! The fuss was getting on Sasha's nerves; he sat in his room feeling angry; but still they talked him into staying and he promised to leave no earlier than the first of July.

The time passed quickly. After luncheon on St. Peter's Day Andrei Andreyich went with Nadya to Moscovsky Street to look once more at the house which had been rented and prepared for the young couple some time ago. The house had two stories, but at the moment only the upper one was decorated. In the large reception room the highly polished floor had been painted to imitate parquet; there were Viennese chairs, a grand piano and a music stand for the violin. There was a smell of paint. On the wall, in a golden frame, hung a large oil painting of a naked lady beside a violet-colored vase with its handle broken off.

"What a wonderful picture!" said Andrei Andreyich and took a deep breath out of respect. "It's by the artist Shishmachevsky."

Beyond was the drawing room with a round table, a sofa and armchairs upholstered in a bright blue material. Above the sofa was a large photographic portrait of Father Andrei wearing his tall cylindrical hat and all his orders. Then they went into the dining room with its buffet, and afterwards into the bedroom. Here two beds stood side by side in the half-darkness, and it looked just as if the bedroom had been furnished with the idea in mind that things would always be very nice here and could not possibly be otherwise. Andrei Andreyich led Nadya through the rooms, holding her round the waist all the time. She, for her part, felt weak and guilty; she hated all these rooms, beds and easy chairs, and the naked lady made her feel sick. It was plain to her by now that she no longer loved Andrei Andreyich or, perhaps, never had loved him; but she did not see, she could not see, how she was going to say this, nor to whom, nor what would be the use of saying it anyway, though she thought about it day and night . . . He held her round the waist, spoke so tenderly, so humbly, and was so happy strutting about his apartment. But she saw nothing in all this but vulgarity, stupid, naïve, insufferable vulgarity, and his arm embracing her waist seemed to her as hard and cold as an iron hoop. At any moment she was ready to run away, to burst into tears, to throw herself out of the window. Andrei Andreyich led her into the bathroom, and there he reached out for a faucet

that was fixed to the wall, and water immediately
flowed out.

"What do you think of that?" he said and burst out
laughing. "I ordered a two-hundred-and-fifty gallon
tank put in the attic, and now you and I will have running water."

They walked up and down the courtyard and then
went out into the street where they took a cab. Thick
clouds of dust filled the air, and it looked as if it were
just about to rain.

"You're not cold, are you?" asked Andrei Andrevich,
screwing up his eyes against the dust.

She said nothing.

"Yesterday, you remember, Sasha reproached me
for doing nothing," he said, after a brief silence. "No
doubt about it, he's right! Absolutely right! I don't do
anything and I can't do anything. Why is that, my
darling? Why is even the very thought of going into
Government service and sticking a cockade in my
cap so abhorrent to me? Why do I feel so uncomfortable when I see a lawyer, or a teacher of Latin, or a
member of the Town Council? Oh, Mother Russia!
Oh, Mother Russia! How many idle, useless people
you bear on your bosom! How many you have like me,
my long-suffering country!"

And he made a generalization from the fact that he
himself did nothing, and saw in it a sign of the times.

"When we are married," he went on, "we'll move to

the country, dearest, we'll work there! We'll buy ourselves a little plot of land with a garden and a stream,
we'll work hard and observe life . . . Oh, how grand
it will be!"

He took off his hat and his hair waved in the wind,
but she listened and thought, Oh God, I want to go
home! Oh God! When they were almost at her house
they overtook Father Andrei.

"There's my father!" said Andrei Andreyich joyfully and began waving his hat. "I love my old dad, I
really do," he said, as he paid off the driver. "He's a
fine old man, a kind old man."

Nadya went into the house feeling angry and unwell, reflecting that their guests would be there the
whole evening, that she would have to entertain them,
smile, listen to the violin, hear all sorts of rubbish and
talk of nothing but the wedding. Her grandmother,
important-looking and resplendent in her silk gown,
haughty as she always seemed in front of guests, was
sitting by the samovar. Father Andrei came in with his
usual sly smile.

"I have the pleasure and the abundant consolation of
seeing you in good health," he said to the old lady, and
it was hard to guess whether he spoke in jest or in earnest.

The wind beat on the window and on the roof; one
could hear it whining, while in the stove the house-

goblin sang his own plaintive and gloomy little song. It was shortly after midnight. Everyone in the house was in bed by now, but no one was asleep, and Nadya had the feeling all the time that someone was playing the violin downstairs. A sharp bang was heard, a shutter must have broken loose. In a minute Nina Ivanovna came in with a candle, wearing only a night-gown.

"What was that banging, Nadya?" she asked.

With her hair braided into a single plait, and a timid smile, her mother seemed on this stormy night older, plainer, not so tall. Nadya remembered how not so long ago she had thought her mother an extraordinary woman and listened with pride to the words she spoke. But now she could not remember any of those words; everything that came to mind seemed feeble and point-less.

The chanting of several bass voices rang out from the chimney, and it even sounded like: "O-o-o-ohhh, my Go-o-o-od!" Nadya sat up in bed and suddenly clutched hard at her hair and began to sob.

"Oh Mother, Mother," she burst out, "my darling, if you only knew what is the matter with me! I beg you, I implore you, let me go away! I implore you!"

"Where to?" asked Nina Ivanovna, bewildered, and she sat down on the bed. "Go away where?"

Nadya cried for a long time and could not say a word.

"Let me go away from this town!" she said at last. "There mustn't be any wedding and there isn't going to be! Do try to understand! I don't love this man . . . I can't even talk about him."

"No, my child, no," said Nina Ivanovna quickly, terribly frightened. "Calm yourself—you are upset. It will pass. These things happen. You've probably had a quarrel with Andrei, but 'The course of true love never did run smooth.' "

Nadya burst into tears. "Oh, please go away, Mother, go away!"

"Yes," said Nina Ivanovna after a short silence. "Not so long ago you were a baby, and a little girl, and now all at once you are engaged to be married. There is a constant metabolism in Nature. And before you know it you will turn into a mother and an old woman yourself, and have just such an obstinate little daughter of your own as I have."

"My dear, kind mother, you *are* intelligent, you know, you *are* unhappy," said Nadya. "You are very unhappy—so why do you say such dreadfully trite things? In God's name, why?"

Nina Ivanovna wanted to say something, but could not get a word out; she began to sob and went back to her room. The bass voices began droning again in the stove, and it suddenly became frightening. Nadya jumped out of bed and ran quickly to her mother's room. Nina Ivanovna, her face covered with tears, lay in bed covered with a pale-blue blanket, holding a book in her hands.

"Mother, listen to me!" Nadya cried. "I implore you, think it over and try to understand me! Just try to understand how terribly petty and degrading our life is. My eyes have been opened, and I see it all now. And what sort of a man is your Andrei Andreyich? You know he is stupid, Mamma! Good God! Can't you see, Mamma, he's a fool!"

Nina Ivanovna sat up impetuously.

"You and your grandmother are torturing me!" she said, sobbing. "I want to live! To live!" she repeated and struck herself twice on the breast with her small fist. "Give me my freedom! I'm still young, I want to live, and you two have made an old woman out of me!"

She began to cry bitterly, lay down and curled herself up in a ball under the blanket. She looked very small, pitiful and foolish. Nadya went back to her own room, dressed, and sat down at the window and began to wait for morning. She sat there all night lost in thought, while outside someone was continually beating on the shutters and whistling.

In the morning the old lady complained that all the apples in the garden had been blown down by the wind during the night, and one old plum tree had been knocked over. It was so gray, dark and dismal one felt like lighting the lamp; the rain beat on the windows and everyone grumbled about the cold. Nadya went to Sasha's room after tea and without saying a word fell on her knees beside his armchair and hid her face in her hands.

"What's the matter?" asked Sasha.

"I can't . . ." she said. "I don't understand, I just can't comprehend how I could live here till now! I despise my fiancé, I despise myself, I despise this whole lazy, meaningless life. . . ."

"There, there," said Sasha, still unable to grasp what had happened. "That's all right . . . that's fine."

"This life has become repulsive to me," Nadya went on. "I can't stay here another day. Tomorrow, I'm leaving this place. Take me with you, for God's sake!"

Sasha looked at her for a moment in astonishment. At last he understood and was as delighted as a small child. He waved his hands and began tapping his slippers on the floor as though dancing for joy.

"Magnificent!" he said, rubbing his hands. "Lord, how wonderful this is!"

She stared at him with large, adoring eyes, unblinking, as though under a spell, expecting him at any moment to say something full of significance, infinitely important; he had not said anything to her yet, but already she felt that something new and wide, such as she had never known before, was opening out before her, and already she was gazing at him, filled with anticipation, ready for anything, even unto death.

The Fiancée

"I'm leaving tomorrow," he said after thinking it over a moment, "and you will be going to the train to see me off . . . I'll take your baggage in my own trunk and get a ticket for you; then when the third bell rings, you will step inside the carriage—and we'll just go. You can come with me as far as Moscow, and then go on to Petersburg by yourself. Have you a passport* ?"

"Yes, I have."

"I swear to you you won't be sorry and won't regret it," Sasha said, quite carried away. "You'll go away and study, and then let fate take care of you. When you have transformed your life, then everything else will change. The main thing is—transform your life, and nothing else will matter. So then, this means we're going away tomorrow?"

"Oh yes! For God's sake!"

It seemed to Nadya that she was deeply moved, that her heart was heavy as never before, and that from now until the moment of departure she would suffer and be tortured by her own thoughts. But hardly had she returned to her room upstairs and lain down on her bed when she fell asleep at once and slept soundly, with a smile on her tear-stained face, until the evening.

* This refers to an internal passport, not for travel abroad. Every Russian was required to carry such an identity card at all times when away from home.

They sent for a cab. Nadya, already in her hat and coat, went upstairs to take a last look at her mother, at all her own things; she stood awhile in her room by her bed, which was still warm, looked all around, then went softly into her mother's room. Nina Ivanovna was asleep, it was quiet in the room. Nadya kissed her mother and smoothed her hair, and stood still there a minute or two . . . Then she went slowly back downstairs.

It was raining hard outdoors. The coachman, wet through, stood in front of the doorway with his hood up.

"There isn't room for you to ride with him, Nadya," said her grandmother as the servants began to load on the trunks. "Fancy wanting to see him off in such weather! Better stay at home. Look how it's pouring!"

Nadya wanted to say something but could not. Now Sasha helped Nadya up into the carriage and covered her knees with the lap robe. Then he himself took his place beside her.

"Good luck! God bless you!" her grandmother called from the porch. "And you, Sasha, write to us from Moscow!"

"All right. Good-bye, Babulya!"

"May the Holy Mother keep you!"

"What wretched weather!" said Sasha.

Only now did Nadya begin to cry. It was clear to her now that she really was going away, which she still could not believe while she was saying goodbye to her grandmother, while she was looking at her mother. Farewell, town! And suddenly it all came back to her: Andrei, and his father, and their new apartment, and the naked lady with the vase; and none of it was frightening any longer, none of it oppressive, but only naïve and petty as it was left farther and farther behind. And when they had taken their seats in the railway carriage and the train started, all the past, which had seemed so vast and important before, rolled up into a little ball, and an immense, wide future, which had seemed so small till now, swung round into its place. The rain beat against the carriage windows, only the green fields could be seen, telegraph poles flashed by, with birds on the wires between, and all at once happiness took her breath away. She remembered that she was going away to study, she was going away to freedom, and it was exactly the same as what used to be called in days long gone "running away to the Cossacks.* " She laughed and cried and prayed, all at the same time.

"It's a-a-a-all right!" said Sasha grinning. "It's a-a-a-all right!"

Autumn passed, and winter after it. Nadya was by now very homesick and every day she thought of her

---

* Serfdom was not recognized among the Cossacks, and so many serfs ran away to join them that this phrase became a cliché.

mother and her grandmother, and she thought of Sasha. Peaceful, kindly letters arrived from home and it seemed that all had been forgiven and forgotten. In May, after her examinations, she set out for home, feeling very well and happy, and on her way she stopped in Moscow to see Sasha. He was just the same as last summer, with his beard, his untidy hair, exactly the same frock coat and canvas trousers, exactly the same large, wonderful eyes; but he looked sick and worn, he had aged and grown thin and coughed continually. He appeared to Nadya somehow dreary and provincial.

"Good lord, Nadya has come!" he said and laughed happily. "My dear, my darling!"

They sat a little while in his printing office which was filled with cigarette smoke and smelled strongly, almost suffocatingly, of India ink and printer's ink; afterward they went to his room which was also filled with cigarette smoke and stained with spit. On the table, beside the cold samovar, was a broken plate with a dark fly-paper on it, and there were a lot of dead flies on the table and on the floor. Everything showed very plainly that Sasha managed his personal life sloppily and lived haphazardly, with complete contempt for comfort; and if anyone had tried to speak to him about his personal happiness or his personal life or about loving him, he would not have understood and would only have laughed.

"Don't worry, everything came out all right in the end," Nadya was saying hurriedly. "Mother came to see me in Petersburg in the autumn and said that Babulya wasn't angry, only she kept going to my room and making the sign of the cross on the walls."

Sasha looked cheerful, but he coughed every now and again and spoke in a cracked voice, and Nadya kept looking at him and could not be certain whether he was really seriously ill or only appeared so to her.

"Sasha, darling," she said, "you really *are* sick, aren't you!"

"No, it's nothing much. Sick, but not badly . . ."

"Oh, my God," Nadya said anxiously, "why don't you go and see a doctor, why don't you look after your health? My dear, darling Sasha," she said, and tears sprang to her eyes. For some reason she saw in imagination Andrei Andreyich and the naked lady with the vase, and everything in her recent past which now seemed as far away as her childhood; and the reason she had begun to cry was that Sasha no longer seemed to her as original, brilliant and interesting as he had last year. "Darling Sasha, you are very, very sick. If only I knew what to do for you so you wouldn't look so pale and thin. I owe so much to you! You've no idea how much you've done for me, my dear, kind Sasha! Really and truly, you are the closest, dearest person of all to me now."

They sat and talked for some time. Now, after

Nadya had spent the winter in Petersburg, Sasha—his words, his smile and his whole appearance—had the air of something outworn, old-fashioned, long since finished and done with, and perhaps already marked for the grave.

"The day after tomorrow I'm going to the Volga," said Sasha, "and then for the kumiss. I want to drink some kumiss. One of my friends and his wife are going with me. His wife is a wonderful person; I nag her all the time, trying to persuade her to go away and study. I want her to transform her life."

After they had talked for a while, they went to the station. Sasha treated her to tea and apples; but as he stood there, smiling and waving his handkerchief when the train pulled out, it was obvious even from the way his legs looked that he was very ill and could hardly live much longer.

Nadya arrived at her home town at noon. When she was driving home from the station the streets appeared to her immensely wide, but the houses seemed small and flattened out; there was no one about, and she came across only the German piano tuner in his ginger overcoat. All the houses seemed to be covered with dust. Her grandmother, now looking really old and as fat and ugly as ever, seized Nadya in her arms and cried a long time, pressing her face to Nadya's shoulder, and could not tear herself away. Nina Ivanovna had grown much older and plainer too, she seemed very peaked, but she was still as tightly laced as of old, and diamonds sparkled on her fingers.

"My darling!" she said, trembling all over. "My darling!"

Afterward they sat down and cried without saying anything. It was evident that both her grandmother and her mother felt that their past life had gone forever and was beyond recall. They no longer had their former place in society, nor the honor they had enjoyed in the past, nor the right to invite guests to their house. It was as though in the very midst of someone's easy, carefree life the police had suddenly appeared in the middle of the night, searched the house, and the householder had turned out to be an embezzler and a forger—and goodbye forever then to that easy, carefree life.

Nadya went upstairs and saw the same bed, the same windows with their naïve white curtains, and outside the windows the same garden, flooded with sunlight, gay and noisy. She touched her old desk, sat down awhile and reflected. She had a good dinner and drank tea with delicious rich cream, but still something was missing; there was an emptiness in all the rooms, and the ceilings pressed low. In the evening she went to bed, covered herself up, and somehow it struck her as funny to be lying here in this warm, very soft bed.

Nina Ivanovna came in for a moment and sat down, like a guilty person, timidly and with many backward glances.

"Well, how are you, Nadya?" she asked after a short silence. "Are you happy? Really happy?"

"I am happy, Mother."

Nina Ivanovna stood up and made the sign of the cross over Nadya and over the windows.

"Well, I have become quite religious, as you see," she said. "You know, I am wrapped up in philosophy now and I keep thinking, thinking all the time . . . A great deal has become as clear as day to me now. First of all, it seems to me, the whole of life must pass as through a prism."

"Tell me, Mamma, is Babulya well?"

"She seems to be all right. When you went away with Sasha and your telegram came, the moment your grandmother read it, she fainted; she lay three days without moving. Afterward she cried and prayed to God all the time. But now she is all right."

She stood up and paced up and down the room.

"Click-clack," sounded the watchman. "Click-clack, click-clack. . . ."

"First of all, the whole of life must pass through a prism, as it were," she said. "That is, in other words, life must in consciousness be divided into its simplest elements, rather like the seven basic colors, and each element must be studied separately."

Nadya fell asleep so soon that she never heard what else Nina Ivanovna said nor when she left the room.

May passed, and June came in. Nadya had by now got used to the house. Her grandmother, sighing deeply, busied herself over the samovar; Nina Ivanovna talked about her philosophy in the evenings; she continued to live in the house, as before like a sponger, and she had to ask the old lady for every penny. There were a great many flies in the house, and the ceilings seemed to get lower and lower all the time. Babulya and Nina Ivanovna never went outside for fear they might run into Father Andrei and Andrei Andreyich.

Nadya walked in the garden and around the streets; she looked at the houses and the gray fences, and it seemed to her that everything in the town had grown old and outdated long ago, and that everyone was only waiting for the end or for something fresh and young to begin anew. Oh, if only this new, shining life, when one could look fate boldly in the eye and feel oneself to be right, and be happy and free—if only this life would come faster! And sooner or later such a life would come! Why, the time would come when not even a trace of her grandmother's house would remain, the time would come when no one would remember this house where things were so arranged now that four servants had no other choice but to live in filth in a single basement room. The small children from the neighboring courtyard provided the only diversion for

Nadya; when she strolled in the garden, they would bang on the fence and tease her, laughing.

"Look at the bride! Look at the bride!"

A letter from Sasha arrived from Saratov. He wrote in his gay, dancing hand that the journey down the Volga had been a complete success but that he had been a little unwell at Saratov, had lost his voice and had been in the hospital for the past two weeks. She understood what that meant and was gripped by forebodings almost amounting to a certainty. And it troubled her that these forebodings and thoughts about Sasha did not upset her as much as they had before. She passionately wanted to live, to go away to Petersburg, and her friendship with Sasha now seemed to her very sweet, but far, far in the past! She did not sleep all night, and in the morning she was sitting by the window listening. Now voices could indeed be heard downstairs. Her grandmother, alarmed, began rapidly asking questions about something. Afterwards someone began to cry . . . When Nadya went downstairs, Babulya was standing in the corner praying, and her face was covered with tears. A telegram lay on the table.

Nadya walked up and down the room a long time, listening to her grandmother weeping, then she picked up the telegram and read it. It announced that Alexander Timofeyich, or familiarly Sasha, had died of consumption at Saratov yesterday morning.

Babulya and Nina Ivanovna went off to church to order the office for the dead, while Nadya continued to pace the rooms for a long time, lost in thought. She saw clearly that her life had been transformed, as Sasha had wanted, that she was alone, alien and unneeded here and that nothing here was of any use to her; her whole past had been torn away from her and was gone as though consumed by fire, and the ashes were scattered on the wind. She went into Sasha's room and stood there awhile.

Goodbye, dear Sasha! she thought, and the image of a new, broad and spacious life appeared before her; and this life, still indistinct and full of mystery, beckoned to her and drew her on.

She went upstairs to her room to pack, and on the next morning she said farewell to her family and, joyfully and in high spirits, left the town—as she supposed, forever.

Notes

The Notes to the first five stories are taken directly from
Polnoe Sobranie Sochineniy i Pisem A. P. Chekhova
(20 vols., Moscow) as follows: "Late-Blooming Flowers"
from vol. 1, 1944; "The Little Trick" from vol. 4, 1946;
"Verochka" from vol. 6, 1946; "The Beauties" from
vol. 7, 1947, and "Big Volodya and Little Volodya"
from vol. 8, 1947.

In the case of the last three stories, "A Visit to
Friends," "A Reward Denied," and "The Fiancée," the
Notes are taken from *A. P. Chekhov: Sobranie Sochin-
eniy.* (12 vols., Moscow), all from vol. 8, 1956.

Late-Blooming Flowers

First published in the journal *Mirskoie Tolk* (*Talk of the Town*) in four instalments in 1882: No. 37, October 10, No. 38, October 17, No. 39, October 23 and No. 41, November 11. Signed: A. CHEKHONTA.

In the Central Government Archives of Literature and Art in Moscow two rough author's manuscripts are preserved: one, consisting of one page, contains the beginning of the story; the other, of eighteen pages, corresponds to the first chapter.

The first manuscript is identical to the later beginning, with the exception of three unimportant renderings, but the rough manuscripts of the first chapter of the story differs considerably from the published text.

The story was dedicated to Nikolai Ivanovich Korobov, a close friend of Chekhov in his university days, afterward a doctor. Korobov, while he was a student, once lived with Chekhov's family in Moscow as a boarder. They kept up the friendship and were in correspondence until the end of Chekhov's life.

The Little Trick

First published in the journal *Sverchok* (*The Cricket*), No. 10, March 12, 1886, under the pseudonym A MAN WITH- OUT SPLEEN.

After corrections the story was included by the author in Volume II of his collected works. A substantial number of cuts were made; in particular, one whole episode describing the hero having dinner at Nadyenka's home was omitted. A great many addresses to the reader were cut (for example: "But, dear sirs, women are capable of sacrifice. I am ready to swear to this a thousand times, even in a court of law, or before the author of the new book *On Women*"), and such literary clichés as "in such a frail vessel," "at breakneck speed, like a bullet," "trembles like a leaf," etc.

The ending of the first published text was different. After the words, ". . . Stretches out her hands against the wind . . . ," was:

That is all I need.
I step out from behind the bushes and, before Nadyenka has time to lower her arms and open her mouth in amazement, I run to her . . . But here, with your permission, we get married.

Notes

Having renounced such a completely happy ending of "The Little Trick," Chekhov put into the later edition of the story a deeper theme, the hero's discontent with life and regret for the lost youth of the heart. As a result of the alterations the story was changed, not only in style, but in its moral meaning too.

Verochka

First published in the paper *Novoye Vremya* (*New Times*), No. 3944, February 21, 1887, and signed: AN. CHEKHOV. After changes in punctuation and substitutions of some words, "Verochka" went into the collection *In the Twilight*, published in 1887 by Suvorin, and repeated in subsequent editions from 1888–1899. It was corrected for the collected edition of 1901, from which our text is taken.

"They are praising your 'Verochka' very highly," his brother Alexei informed him (February 28, 1887).

Veteran novelist Dmitri Grigorovich later wrote Chekhov:

"Your stories "Misfortune," "Verochka," "Home" and "On the Road" prove to me something I have known for a long time, i.e., that your horizon takes in the motif of love perfectly, with all its subtlest and most secret manifestations." December 30, 1888

The Beauties

First published in the paper *Novoye Vremya* (*New Times*), No. 4513, September 21, 1888, and signed: AN. CHEKHOV. In its corrected form it went into the collection *By the Way* published by the journal *The Artist* in 1894. It was again corrected for the collected edition of 1901, and the text used here is from this edition.

In making over the 1894 text, Chekhov made corrections in style and shortened it considerably.

For example, ". . . her capricious beauty would float away like the pollen of a flower." was followed originally by ". . . All the passengers were looking at the beauty in silence; only, I remember, some lady behind me said to someone, 'I don't see anything out of the ordinary in her, Sasha; a pretty little thing, that's all.' And a masculine voice answered her, 'That means you don't get the point at all.'"

The autobiographical lines of the story were noted in a letter to Chekhov from his first cousin G. M. Chekhov:

Thank you for the story "The Beauties," which reminded me of your, and my, grandfather, and of the driver Karpo, who also came to our place with grandfather. I remember I used to spend the whole day in the stable around the horses with Karpo, and along with him I would take supper to my father in the store. In that Armenian to whose place you "drove with your grandfather," I at once pictured Nazar Minaich Nazarov, with his insistent and reckless character, pictured him as he used to be when he would come every evening to see my father in the store.

Big Volodya and Little Volodya

First published in the liberal daily newspaper *Russkiye Vedmosti* (*Russian News*), No. 357, December 28, 1893. Signed: ANTON CHEKHOV. It was corrected for the collection *Stories and Tales*, 1894, and corrected once more for the collected works, 1901, from which our text is taken.

When he included the story in the collection of 1894 Chekhov made a number of corrections in the text, and for the collected edition he added a word here and there and also made more cuts in the text. For example, on page 141 after "looked around like a beast of prey." he cut out the following:

How could you have married me, she thought, looking at him with anger, when you know perfectly well you are an old man, older than my father? What right had you? What right? Your money? Eh?

She felt like doing something *par dépit*, something awful, incredible, something that would make trouble for herself and her husband and her father, too, who had so dishonorably given his permission for her marriage. It would make no difference to her, she had nothing to lose: she did not believe in God, and death was still a long way off; but if there should be a God then everlasting torments awaited her, and since her position was hopeless it was just as though she were sinking up to her neck in a quagmire.She could not go into a convent because it was deadly, and really if she had to renounce life altogether it would be better to kill herself, do away with herself in a moment with a knife or poison or a rope, rather than enter a convent.

After the newspaper publication of his story Chekhov wrote V. A. Goltsev, one of the editors:

Ach, my story in *Russian News* has been cut so zealously they have cut off the head along with the hair. The prudery is purely childish, but the cowardice is dumbfounding. Had they cut out a few lines one wouldn't have minded, but they slashed the middle, chewed off the end, and my story is so mangy it really makes me sick. All right, let's assume it is cynical; in that case the editors should either not print it at all, or they should in all fairness have a word with the author or write to him, especially as the story didn't go into the Christmas number but was held off for an indefinite time. December 28, 1893

Chekhov also wrote about the free treatment of the newspaper edition to his French translator, Jules Legras:

If by any chance you have already translated "Big Volodya and Little Volodya," please don't be in any hurry to print it. The fact is that the editors of *Russian News* have left many things out of this story, out of prudery and cowardice. I will, without fail, send you the story *in toto*. March 27, 1894

A Visit to Friends

First published in the journal *Cosmopolis*, Vol. IX, No. 2, February, 1898.

The Institute of Russian Literature (Pushkin House), Academy of Sciences, Moscow, holds the author's manuscript of the story signed: ANTON CHEKHOV. It consists of twenty-four pages, written on one side only; the tenth page has been lost. A comparison of the journal text with the manuscript shows that Chekhov made a number of small corrections.

On April 16, 1897, F. D. Batyushkov, who had taken over the publication of the Russian section of *Cosmopolis,* then being published in four languages, asked Chekhov for his collaboration. Chekhov answered on April 21 and agreed to send a story, but not before the autumn. On December 15, Chekhov wrote to Batyushkov from Nice:

I am working on the story for *Cosmopolis,* writing with some difficulty, and in snatches. I usually write slowly and with effort, but here in my hotel room, at someone else's desk, in lovely weather that draws one out of doors, it is even more difficult to write—that's why I can't promise you the story for another two weeks. I will send it before January 1st, and then please be kind enough to send me back the proofs, which I shall only keep a day. So you can count on publishing it in your February edition, but no earlier.

Notes

At the end of his letter Chekhov wrote:

You expressed a desire in one of your letters for me to send you an international story, taking something from the local life as a topic. I could only write a story like that in Russia, from memory. I can only write from memory, I have never written directly from life. I have always had to strain a subject through my memory so that in it, as in a filter, only what was important or typical remained.

The story was finished at the beginning of January, 1898. On January 3, when he sent it to Batyushkov, Chekhov wrote:

. . . I am sending you the manuscript. Please send me back the proofs because my story is not yet finished and will only be ready when I have made dirty marks all over the proofs. I can only give it the finishing touches in proof, in the manuscript I never see anything.

The proofs were sent to Chekhov in Nice on January 15. He received them on the nineteenth and returned them to Batyushkov on January 23. In his letter to A. S. Suvorin, editor of the Moscow journal *New Times*, Chekhov wrote with great displeasure:

Several days ago I read on the front page of *New Times* a pop-eyed advertisement about the publication of my story "On a Visit." Firstly, I didn't write "On a Visit," but "A Visit to Friends." Secondly, such an advertisement jars on me; moreover, the story is far from pop-eyed, it is the sort of thing that gets written one a day. February 6, 1898

A Reward Denied

This work of Chekhov's was never finished. Notations and corrections appear on the manuscript, evidently in the hand of V. S. Mirolyubov, the editor of *Zhurnal dlya Vsyokh* (*Journal for Everyone*), in which the unfinished story was published posthumously (No. 2, 1905). The story was probably intended by Chekhov for *Journal for Everyone*, and should be dated from the year of his collaboration on the magazine, 1902–1903.

The Fiancée

First published in *Journal for Everyone,* No. 12, December 1903. It was included by the author in Volume XII of his collected works, 1903, as well as in the posthumous edition of 1906.

Chekhov began to work on this, his last story in 1902. On October 20, in answer to a question from the editor of the magazine, V. S. Mirolyubov, he wrote, "If you must have the name of the story, which I may have to change later, then here it is: "Nevesta" (The Fiancée). . . . Don't be angry. I will write the story." It was not finished until February 27, 1903, a week or two after he had begun work on his last work, *The Cherry Orchard.*

When he sent off the manuscript that day from Yalta to the editor, Chekhov wrote, "Please return the proofs, for I have to correct them and work on the ending. I always work on the endings in proof." He read over the proofs of his story in May, when the increasing severity of his illness made work slow and difficult for him, and on the fifth of June he wrote to his friend V. V. Veresaev: "I have scribbled corrections all over 'The Fiancée' and finished it off in proof." On June 12, when he returned the proofs to Mirolyubov, editor of *Journal for Everyone,* Chekhov informed him: "I have today returned a package of printed matter to you. Please forgive me, I had nothing to do, so in my leisure I was carried away and wrote the whole story by hand." And in a further letter of July 2, Chekhov wrote him: "I sent you back the proofs a long time ago; please be good enough to let me have them back once more so I can glance over them—not for corrections, but for the punctuation marks!" On July 6, Mirolyubov replied: "Thank you very much for the proofs. As for the corrections, we shall leave that to you."

In the Manuscript Division of the Lenin Library, Moscow, is the author's rough manuscript of the story with a great many corrections, deletions and insertions. The clean manuscript of "The Fiancée" has not come down to us, but there are galleys of the first and second proofs, which Chekhov kept at the time his story was published in *Journal for Everyone*. They are now in the Institute of Russian Literature (Pushkin House), Academy of Sciences, Moscow. The text printed in the first proofs, evidently taken from a clean manuscript unknown to us, differs considerably from the text of the rough manuscript. Chekhov made a great many changes and additions to his characters, especially to "the fiancée" herself, and to Sasha; he also made major changes in style.

In Chapter 2, for instance, the rough manuscript reads:

"Mamma darling, why am I so unhappy?" she asked after waiting a few moments, and tears came to her eyes. "It seems to me it's because I have nothing to do."

"Well, really, what is there to do here?" said her mother spiritedly. "Your darling grandmother takes everything into her own hands and I don't even dare pour out my own tea. I know it's boring for you without occupation, but you could never convince your grandmother of that."

Nadya put her arm round her mother and they walked along together in silence.

"But you could paint, couldn't you?" said Nina Ivanovna. "Or sew?"

"Why should I sew? Why should I paint?"

Her mother did not answer. Nadya felt for some reason disappointed, and she suddenly began to cry.

"Oh, don't pay any attention to me, Mamma," she said. "I am just not in spirits today."

After reading the second proofs Chekhov again made major cuts and changes, especially in Chapters 3 and 6. However, the magazine text differs in several places from the corrected text of the second proofs. Evidently Chekhov read the story a third time in proofs which have not come down to us.

Thus, for example, in Chapter 3, after the words ". . . they gave her grandmother Lenten borsch," in the second proofs there is the following passage:

Nina Ivanovna, who was always under treatment for something, was given bouillon, and Sasha and Nadya meat soup with pickled cucumbers.

"They say they are going to make our town the governor's headquarters," said the old lady.

"They want to make a capital city out of your town!" said Sasha with an ironical grin.

"It's not only our town, it's your town too. Remember you were born here."

"It's a splendid city!" went on Sasha ironically. "There isn't a single shopkeeper who doesn't cheat, not one civil servant who isn't prematurely bald from card-playing or vodka. Out of doors it's filthy dusty and it stinks. They borrow money and don't pay it back; they take your books and don't return them . . . *Canaille!*"

"He's rambling on and on and he doesn't know what he's talking about," said the grandmother, sighing deeply.

She loved Sasha and was sorry for him, but she suspected that he got drunk and played cards himself in Moscow and that that was why he was sick; and whenever he brought the subject up, she sighed deeply every time.

"The town's dead, the people in it are dead," went on Sasha, "and if, let's say, it were to collapse in ruins it would be written up in all the papers in three short lines and no one would cry about it."

Silence followed. They served bream stuffed with kasha to the grandmother, and to the rest chicken gravy.

"It's a backward town," Sasha began again, "a crude, ignorant town. Bismarck said, 'Slow to saddle, but swift in travel, is the character of the Russian.' But to tell the truth, this town hasn't made up its mind to saddle yet."

This was all cut from the third proof, evidently, and in the magazine text nothing was left in except "bream stuffed with kasha."

In Chapter 6, big changes were made. Chekhov deleted from the second proofs the following passage, occurring after "Why ever don't you take care of yourself?"

"And as usual you're sloppily dressed, your hair is messy, you ought to be ashamed of yourself! Whyever should it be this way with us, that to be a good man you have to dress badly, neglect your health . . . ? Why?"

"Ha, ha, ha!" Sasha began to laugh.

"I'm going to take you away with me today. Pack your things!"

"That's impossible," said Sasha, laughing. "I will join you next year, but now we're leaving for the Volga tomorrow, another fellow and I. He's a nice fellow, only a bit odd. You say to him, let's assume, 'I'm hungry,' 'I'm deeply insulted,' 'I'm completely crushed,' 'We are degenerating,' and in reply he explains to me about the Grand Inquisitor, about Zossima, about mystical attitudes—and all because he's afraid to give a straight answer to a question. To give a straight answer—that would be terrible! It's just like a babel of many tongues. One man asks, 'Give me an axe,' and the other answers, 'Go to hell!' "

"What a lot of rubbish," said Nadya tearfully. "You are leaving with me today, or you'll die here! Just look at yourself!"

Later on Nadya calmed down a little; they talked about Petersburg, and about her new life, and Sasha took her all the way to the station and was very happy.

"It's perfect, it's superb!" he said. "I'm very happy. You won't be sorry and you won't regret it, I swear to you. Even if you have to be sacrificed, still, without sacrifice nothing is possible, without the lowest step there would be no staircase. Our grand-children and great-grandchildren will thank you for it."

But the theme of "sacrifice" and Nadya's departure for revolutionary work were deleted from the second proof.

In his reminiscences of Chekhov, V. V. Veresaev tells the following story:

We were at Gorky's reading the proofs of Chekhov's new story, "The Fiancée."
Anton Pavlovich asked, "Well, how do you like the story?"
I hesitated but decided to speak frankly.
"Anton Pavlovich, girls don't run off to a revolution in this way. And girls like your Nadya aren't going to join any revolution."
His eyes took on a stern, watchful expression.
"There are many different ways there."

A great many opinions appeared in the press remarking on the courageous theme and attitude of the new story, and it was considered a very striking turning point in Chekhov's work.

V. Botsyanovsky in *Russ'* (*Russia*), No. 22, January 1904, in "Chekhov's New Story," considered the story as a "land-mark," and as evidence of a turning point in Russian litera-ture towards "the new and the bright." "Of all the earlier heroes of Chekhov," the critic wrote, "not one ever allowed himself to take such resolute steps, and by now the flight of Nadya to her studies may be recognized as a new stage in Chekhov's work as a writer."

A. I. Bogdanovich in *Mir Bozhii* (*The World*), No. 1, 1904, under "A. B.—Critical Notes" wrote:

"The Fiancée"—that delightful, beautifully written work which seems to us a symbol of profound significance . . . The courageous, powerful chord which ends this fascinating work resounds in the heart of the reader like a triumphant war cry, like the triumph of life over the tedium of death and gray banality and monotonous habit. . . . Chekhov's "Fiancée"— that living and shining symbol of everything that is alive and protesting, not confined within the out-of-date limits of gray provincial life . . . Nadya and her friends, everyone who decides to transform his life, all bear within them a new culture, a new foundation for "grandmother's house," to which they bring bright hopes, a desire to rebuild the house quite differently, and the knowledge how it is to be done.

M. Voloshin, *Kievskii Otkliki* (*Comments from Kiev*), January 8, 1904, in "Literary Characteristics," wrote:

Outwardly this is a typical Chekhovian story, written in a gentle tone and drawing most carefully, in tender, elegiac colors with fine nuances in construction and in a very few lines, whole categories of types and characteristic traits of the moment.

But in Sasha's words to Nadya, the critic found a profound significance.

In those burning words, you discern the Chekhovian themes: His implacable hostility toward the bourgeois nest, where everything and everyone are so much alike, whose ruin none would mourn and none would regret. ["My Life."] And here is the exuberant call toward the future, full of prophetic enthusiasm —"A glorious future," so glorious it seems unattainable, so unattainable it seems glorious. ["The Black Monk."] To leave the town behind—that means to leave behind the idea of selfish egotism, of parasitism with its greasy gluttony, the little nothings of life and a life of little nothings—and to set out on the broad, shining highway of your favorite, chosen cause.

About the Translators

Dr. I. C. Chertok was born in Nizhni-Novgorod (now Gorky) in 1889. Upon his graduation from high school, he later on moved to Moscow, where he continued his studies in the field of liberal arts, followed by specialized railroad engineering education in the Moscow Engineering Institute, from which he graduated with distinction. While working as a railroad constructional engineer, he traveled the length and breadth of Russia, often living a pioneer life in remote country. During his travels he had the opportunity of becoming familiar with a good number of regional dialects, which proved invaluable to him in his later work as a translator.

In 1932 he was appointed special representative for several large American corporations in the Middle East, where he worked until 1943. He then emigràted to the United States and began teaching in the Russian Department of the School for Oriental Languages at the

University of Colorado. Upon the liquidation of this school following the end of World War II, he was transferred to Washington, D.C., where he continued teaching as assistant professor of Russian.

Since his retirement a few years ago, he has been teaching and translating extensively in and outside New York, earning the well-deserved praise of the educational institutions and of his numerous students who had taken up Russian along with their other studies in the humanities and the sciences.

Jean Gardner was born in Tunbridge Wells, Kent, England, in 1923 and educated at the Reigate County School for Girls in Surrey. During the Second World War she served as a radar operator with the women's branch of the RAF. She came to New York in 1947 and now lives in Nyack with her husband and three children; she has been studying Russian with Mr. Chertok for the last five years.